Ribsy robs The poLice

Cautiously Ribsy approached the open door of the car.

"You get away from there," yelled Henry.

Ribsy jumped into the police car again.

"Ribsy!" Henry called desperately.

Ribsy jumped out of the police car. In his mouth was a brown paper bag.

Henry groaned. A dog that robs police cars! Now he really was in trouble. "Ribsy, you drop that!" he ordered.

Obediently Ribsy dropped the bag. He looked at Henry, wagged his tail, and tore open the bag with his paws and teeth.

Enjoy all of
Beverly Cleary's books

Beverly Cleary

Henry and Ribsy

ILLUSTRATED BY
Tracy Dockray

HarperTrophy®
An Imprint of HarperCollinsPublishers

Henry and Ribsy
Copyright © 1954, renewed 1982 by Beverly Cleary
All rights reserved. Printed in the United States of
America. No part of this book may be used or reproduced
in any manner whatsoever without written permission
except in the case of brief quotations embodied in critical
articles and reviews. For information address
HarperCollins Children's Books, a division of
HarperCollins Publishers, 10 East 53rd Street,
New York, NY 10022.
www.harpercollinschildrens.com

Library of Congress Catalog Card Number: 54-6402
ISBN-13: 978-0-06-204059-6

Typography by Amy Ryan

❖

Reillustrated Harper Trophy edition, 2007
12 13 CG/BR 10 9 8 7 6 5 4 3

Contents

1

Ribsy and The Lube Job

One warm Saturday morning in August, Henry Huggins and his mother and father were eating breakfast in their square white house on Klickitat Street. Henry's dog Ribsy sat close to Henry's chair, hoping for a handout. While Mr. and Mrs. Huggins listened to the nine o'clock news on the radio, Henry tried to think of something interesting he could do that day. Of course he could

play ball with Scooter or ride his bicycle over to Robert's house and work on the model railroad, but those were things he could do every day. Today he wanted to do something different, something he had never done before.

Before Henry thought of anything interesting to do, the radio announcer finished the news and four men began to sing. Henry, who heard this program every Saturday, sang with them.

"*Woofies Dog Food is the best,*
Contains more meat than all the rest.
So buy your dog a can today
And watch it chase his blues away.
Woof, woof, woof, Woofies!"

Then the sound of a dog barking came out of the radio.

"R-r-r-wuf!" said Ribsy, looking at the radio.

The announcer's voice cut in. "Is your dog a member of the family?" he asked.

"He sure is!" exclaimed Henry to the

radio. "He's the best dog there is."

"Henry, for goodness' sake, turn that down," said Mrs. Huggins, as she poured herself a cup of coffee. "And by the way, Henry, speaking of good dogs reminds me that Mrs. Green said Ribsy ran across the new lawn she just planted. She said he left deep paw prints all the way across."

"Aw, he didn't mean to hurt her old lawn. He was just . . ." Henry remembered that Ribsy had run across the lawn because he was chasing the Grumbies' cat. "He was just in a hurry," he finished lamely. "You're a good dog, aren't you, Ribsy?"

Thump, thump, thump went Ribsy's tail on the rug.

"We think he's a good dog, but the neighbors won't if he runs across new lawns and chases cats," said Mr. Huggins.

Henry looked sharply at his father and wondered how he knew about Ribsy's chasing the Grumbies' cat. At the same time he couldn't see why Ribsy was to blame about the lawn. The cat ran across it first, didn't she? "Well, anyway, Ribsy doesn't keep everybody awake barking at night, like that collie in the next block," said Henry.

"Just the same, you better keep an eye on him. We don't want him to be a nuisance to the neighbors." Mr. Huggins laid his napkin beside his plate. "Well, I guess I'll take the car down to the service station for a lube job."

That gave Henry an idea. Here was his chance to do something he had never done before, something he had always wanted to do when his father had the car greased.

"Oh, boy, I . . ." Henry paused because it occurred to him that his mother might not like his idea. He had better wait and ask his father when they got to the service station. "Can I go?" he asked eagerly.

"Sure," answered Mr. Huggins. "Come along."

"Woofies Dog Food is the best," sang Henry, as he and Ribsy climbed into the front seat of the car. Henry sat in the middle beside his father, because Ribsy liked to lean out the window and sniff all the interesting smells. Henry was happy to be going someplace, even just to the service station, with his father. He always had a grown-up, man-to-man feeling when they were alone together. He wished his father had time to take him places more often.

As they drove toward the service station they passed the Rose City Sporting Goods Shop, where Henry noticed the windows filled with tennis rackets, golf clubs, and fishing tackle. Fishing tackle—that gave Henry a second idea. "Say, Dad," he said, "I was wondering if you plan to go fishing pretty soon."

"I expect I will." Mr. Huggins stopped at a red light. "Hector Grumbie and I thought we'd go salmon fishing sometime in September. Why?"

"How about taking me along this year?" Henry tried to sound grown-up and casual.

Mr. Huggins drove past the supermarket and turned into Al's Thrifty Service Station. "We'll see," he said.

Boy, oh, boy, thought Henry, as he and Ribsy got out of the car near the grease rack. When his father said, "We'll see," he meant, "Yes, unless something unusual happens." If he had said, "Ask your mother," it would mean he didn't care whether Henry went fishing or not. But—"We'll see!" Henry could see himself sitting in a boat reeling in a salmon—a chinook salmon. He could see himself having his picture taken beside his fish and could hear people saying, "Yes, this is Henry Huggins, the boy who caught the enormous chinook salmon."

When Mr. Huggins had arranged with Al, the owner of the station, to have the car lubricated, he turned to Henry and said, "I have to go to the bank and do a few errands. Are you coming with me or do you want to wait here?"

Henry had been so busy thinking about fishing that he had almost forgotten why he came to the filling station in the first place. He looked at the car beside the grease rack and hesitated. Maybe it was a silly idea. Still, it was something he had always wanted to do. "Say . . . uh, Dad, do you suppose I could stay in the car and ride up on the grease rack?"

Mr. Huggins and Al both laughed. "You know, I always wanted to do the same thing when I was a kid," said Mr. Huggins. "It's all right with me, but maybe Al won't think it's such a good idea."

"It's OK with me," said Al, "but once you

get up there you'll have to stay till I finish the job. It may take a while because I have to wait on customers."

"Sure, I'll stay," agreed Henry.

"And you're not to open the car door while you're up there," cautioned Henry's father.

"I won't," promised Henry, and got back into the car. Al drove it onto the rack and then got out to fix the axle supports that held the car to the rack. He turned a handle and Henry felt the car begin to rise.

"So long, Dad," Henry called, as he and the car rose slowly into the air. He felt as if he were riding in an elevator that didn't have a building around it. Too bad some of the boys and girls were not around to see him now.

The car stopped and Henry could hear the pish-tush, pish-tush of the grease gun as Al worked beneath him. How different things

looked from up in the air. And wouldn't it be fun if cars could take off and drive along just this high!

"Wuf!" said Ribsy, looking anxiously up at Henry as if he could not understand what the Huggins car was doing up in the air.

"It's all right, Ribsy," said Henry. "I won't go any higher."

Thump, thump, thump went Ribsy's tail on the cement.

Al left the grease rack to sell some gasoline and check someone's oil. Ribsy, seeing that the car was not going to leave without him, wandered around the service station sniffing the gasoline pumps and the Coke machine. Henry sat behind the steering wheel and pretended he was driving the car around in the air. He wished some of his friends would come along.

Then Scooter McCarthy rode into the service station on his bicycle. He stopped by the air hose and started to unscrew the valve cap on his front tire.

"Hi, Scooter," Henry called.

Startled, Scooter looked around but did not see Henry. He looked puzzled as he bent over to put air into his bicycle tire.

I bet I can have some fun with old Scooter, thought Henry. Then he said in a hollow voice, "I am the ghost of Henry Huggins." Quickly he ducked down in the seat of the car.

The air stopped hissing into Scooter's tire.

Henry peeked out to see Scooter looking worried. "I have come to haunt you," said Henry in his hollow voice, and let out a groan.

"You all right up there, sonny?" asked Al, who had returned from the gasoline pump.

Henry had to answer. "Sure, I'm all right," he said, feeling foolish.

"Aw, I knew you were up there all the

time," said Scooter, unscrewing the valve cap on his back tire.

"You did not," answered Henry. "You just wish you'd thought of riding up on the grease rack."

"Ha," scoffed Scooter, as the air hissed into his tire.

"You know what?" said Henry. "My dad's going to take me salmon fishing this year." That ought to impress Scooter.

"Haven't you ever been fishing?" said Scooter.

"Sure I've been fishing, but not salmon fishing," said Henry. Well, he had been fishing. Once he and his mother and father had picnicked beside the Sandy River when the smelt were running. The river was so thick with the little fish that people dipped them out of the water with nets. Henry did not have a net, but he used an old stocking cap to scoop up some fish. His mother had cooked them for dinner so it really counted as fishing, even though he didn't intend to let Scooter know exactly how he had caught the fish.

"My dad took me salmon fishing last year," boasted Scooter.

Henry might have known Scooter had already gone salmon fishing. He was two years older and always got to do things first. "Catch anything?" Henry asked.

"A silverside," answered Scooter proudly, as he screwed the valve cap back on his wheel.

"Aw, that's just a little salmon," said Henry.

"I don't call fifteen pounds so little," said Scooter.

"I bet I catch a chinook," boasted Henry.

"Ha, I'd like to see you," sneered Scooter. "Why, they weigh twenty or thirty pounds. You couldn't land a chinook even if you did get one to bite."

"I could too land one," said Henry.

"No, you couldn't. I know. I've been salmon fishing and you haven't," Scooter said. Then he called, "So long," and pedaled away.

"You just wait. I will too catch a salmon," yelled Henry.

That old Scooter, he thought. He needn't think he's so smart just because he got to go fishing first.

Al gave the car a few more pish-tushes with the grease gun and hurried off to sell some more gas. Ribsy looked up at Henry as if he wished he would come down.

"Pretty soon, fellow," said Henry, wishing something would happen. Sitting up on the grease rack wasn't as much fun as he had thought it would be.

While Henry was wishing something would happen, a police car stopped in front of the supermarket next door to the service station. The officer got out and hurried into the market.

Boy, oh, boy, thought Henry. Now something is happening. Maybe somebody's holding up the supermarket. If he comes out shooting, I better duck.

"Three M eighty-five, stand by," blared the radio in the police car.

Jeepers, thought Henry, I bet that means headquarters is going to send help. If the burglars get out and try to escape, I'm in a good place to watch where they go. Yes, sir, it's a good thing I'm up here. I'll be a lookout and keep my eagle eye on the door just in case any suspicious-looking people come out.

Henry slid down in the seat and peered over the edge of the car door with his eagle eye. He saw a lady with a baby in a Taylor-tot come out of the supermarket. She was followed by a man on crutches. They didn't look the least bit suspicious. Wait a minute, thought Henry. That man on crutches. Maybe the crutches are a disguise. Maybe when he gets around the corner he'll throw them away and begin to run. I better watch him.

Pish-tush went the grease gun.

"Thirteen L ten meet thirteen A nine," blared the radio in the police car. Here comes help, thought Henry.

Just at that moment Ribsy pointed his nose into the air and sniffed. Then he trotted purposefully toward the police car. Now what's Ribsy up to, wondered Henry, forgetting to keep his eagle eye on the man on crutches. The officer had not slammed the door of the police car shut when he got out. Henry was horrified to see Ribsy push it wider open with his nose and jump into the front seat.

"Here, Ribsy," Henry called. "You get out of there!"

The radio suddenly blared forth. "Three M eighty-five, Second and Broadway."

Frightened, Ribsy scrambled out of the car. The radio was silent.

"You stay away from that police car," ordered Henry from the grease rack.

Cautiously Ribsy approached the open door of the car.

"You get away from there," yelled Henry.

Ribsy jumped into the police car again.

"Ribsy!" Henry called desperately.

Ribsy jumped out of the police car. In his mouth was a brown paper bag.

Henry groaned. A dog that robs police cars! Now he really was in trouble. "Ribsy, you drop that!" he ordered.

Obediently Ribsy dropped the bag. He looked at Henry, wagged his tail, and tore open the bag with his paws and teeth.

Henry looked down at the pavement. It was too far to jump. Anyway, he had promised his father he wouldn't open the car door. There must be some way he could attract attention. "Say, mister," he called to Al, who was working under the car.

Pish-tush went the grease gun. Pish-tush, pish-tush.

"Ribsy!" yelled Henry. The dog looked up and wagged his tail. He had a sandwich in his mouth.

"Drop that!" ordered Henry. Ribsy swallowed the sandwich in two gulps and poked his nose into the paper bag again.

Henry hoped the policeman would stay in the supermarket a long time. He didn't want him to see the thief who had stolen his lunch. Thinking it must be nearly time for his father to return, Henry looked anxiously up and down the street.

Two cars drove into the station, and Al hurried away to sell some more gasoline. Ribsy rolled what looked like a deviled egg out on the sidewalk. He sniffed it and then gobbled it up.

How do you like that, thought Henry. At home he doesn't like the eggs he's supposed to eat to make his coat glossy. Ribsy poked his nose into the bag once more. Henry wondered what happened to dogs that stole lunches, especially policemen's lunches.

At that moment the policeman came out of the supermarket with a bag in his hand. He looked at the open door of his car. Then he saw Ribsy. "Here, you!" he shouted.

What's he going to do to Ribsy? Henry wondered in alarm.

Looking guilty, Ribsy picked up the paper bag and ran between the gasoline pumps. The policeman ran after him. "Come back here," he yelled, and tripped on the hose from the pump. Ribsy ran under the car that was getting gas. "Come out from under there," ordered the policeman.

Al hung the hose on the pump, and the driver of the car started the motor. The sound frightened Ribsy into running out.

I sure wish I could get out of here,

thought Henry. Why doesn't Dad hurry up and come back?

"I'll head him off," Al called to the officer.

Ribsy, followed by Al and the policeman, ran around behind the station, where Henry could not see him. He listened to two pairs of feet running back and forth on the cement and wondered desperately what would happen next. Ribsy appeared from behind the station and raced around to the air and water hoses, where he dropped the bag and looked at the policeman. Henry did not know whether to yell or just slide down in the car and hide.

When the policeman was within a few feet of him, Ribsy picked up the bag, dashed past its owner, and ran under the grease rack. As the policeman ran after him, Henry was horrified to see him put his hand on the gun on his hip.

"Don't shoot," begged Henry. "Please don't shoot my dog!"

Surprised, the policeman stopped alongside of the grease rack and looked all around to see where the voice was coming from.

"I'm up here," said Henry in a small voice. "Please don't shoot my dog. I know he shouldn't have stolen your lunch, but please don't shoot him."

The policeman looked startled to see Henry peering out of the car above his head. "I'm not going to shoot your dog," he said kindly. "I'm just trying to get my lunch back if there's anything left of it."

"I saw you put your hand on your gun and I thought . . ." Henry began.

"I was just trying to keep it from flopping against me when I ran," explained the officer.

Just the same, Henry could not help feeling Ribsy had had a narrow escape. "I'm afraid there isn't much left of your lunch, sir," said Henry politely.

Then, to Henry's relief, Mr. Huggins returned. "What's the trouble?" he wanted to know, when he saw the policeman talking to Henry.

"I just stepped into the market to buy a pint of milk to drink with my lunch," began the officer, and went on to explain what had happened.

A pint of milk! There hadn't been a holdup at all. Henry was disappointed to learn that the policeman had been on such an uninteresting errand—an old pint of milk. Well, he supposed policemen had to drink milk like anyone else.

Mr. Huggins snapped his fingers at Ribsy, who came out from under the grease rack. Looking guilty, he dropped the tattered bag at Mr. Huggins's feet. Part of a cupcake rolled out onto the cement.

"Not much left, is there?" said Mr. Huggins. Then he looked at Ribsy. "Aren't you ashamed of yourself?"

Ribsy's tail and ears drooped. Henry could see his dog really was ashamed. He hoped the policeman noticed how sorry he looked. "What happens to dogs that rob police cars?" Henry asked. "Do they get arrested or get a ticket or something?"

The policeman laughed. "No, nothing like that. But he'll probably get a stomachache from eating too much."

Henry was so relieved to know nothing serious would happen to Ribsy that he was able to grin at the officer. "And it'll serve him right if he does get a stomachache," he said.

After Mr. Huggins had insisted on paying for the lunch, the officer drove away and Al lowered the car. "You old dog," said Henry crossly as Ribsy jumped into the front seat. "Look at the trouble you got me into. And now you've got grease on your tail. Mom isn't going to like that." But when Ribsy looked up at Henry and wagged his tail as if he wanted to be forgiven, Henry could not help patting him.

Mr. Huggins looked thoughtful. "It seems to me that dog has been getting into a lot of trouble lately," he remarked.

"I know he has, but he's still a pretty good dog," said Henry.

On the way home the sight of the Rose City Sporting Goods Shop reminded Henry of salmon fishing once more. "Say, Dad," he said, "I was talking to Scooter McCarthy. He went fishing last year and caught a silverside. I bet I land a chinook. I bet—"

"Wait a minute," interrupted Mr. Huggins. "I didn't say for sure I'd take you fishing. I said, 'We'll see.'"

"Aw, Dad," protested Henry, "that's just the same as yes."

Mr. Huggins was silent a minute before he went on. "You know, Henry, I've been thinking it over and I'll tell you what I'll do. I'll make a bargain with you about the fishing trip."

"What kind of a bargain?" Henry asked, wondering what his father had in mind. He hoped it wasn't anything too hard, because he wanted very much to go on that fishing trip.

"If you keep Ribsy out of trouble between now and the time I go salmon fishing around the middle of September, I'll take you along," said Mr. Huggins. "And that means no complaints from the neighbors about him."

"Sure!" exclaimed Henry. "It's a bargain!" So that was all his father wanted! Why, it would be easy as pie. He didn't have a thing to worry about. All he had to do was keep his eye on his dog from now until the middle

of September, less than two months. He patted Ribsy, who was leaning out the front window of the car. "You're going to be a good dog from now on, aren't you?"

Ribsy wagged his greasy tail in Henry's face. "Wuf!" he said.

"That's a good dog," said Henry. He was sure he wouldn't have any trouble keeping his bargain. If he watched Ribsy every minute, he couldn't get into trouble, could he? Or could he? There was the time Ribsy ran off with the roast the neighbors were going to barbecue in the backyard. And the time he stole the seventeen newspapers Scooter McCarthy had delivered on Klickitat Street. Maybe keeping Ribsy out of trouble until the middle of September wasn't going to be so easy after all, now that he stopped to think about it. And the more Henry thought about it, the more he wished he hadn't been in such a hurry to tell Scooter he was going fishing.

2
Henry and The Garbage

Two weeks before school started, Henry Huggins was in the kitchen one evening feeding Ribsy, while Mr. Huggins washed the dinner dishes and Mrs. Huggins wiped them. Henry took some horse meat and half a can of Woofies Dog Food out of the refrigerator. Thump, thump, thump went Ribsy's tail on the floor as he watched Henry.

Henry cut up the horse meat and put it on Ribsy's dish. "Why don't you chew it?" he asked, when Ribsy began to gulp down the pieces of meat.

Henry spooned the last of the can of Woofies into the plastic dish with D O G printed on it. Ribsy sniffed at the food. Then he wagged his tail and looked hopefully at Henry, who knew this meant that Ribsy would eat the dog food only when he was sure he was not going to get any more horse meat.

"That's all," said Henry. "Eat your Woofies like a good dog. A Woofies dog is a happy dog. See, it says so right here on the can."

"Wuf," said Ribsy, and went to the refrigerator to show that what he really wanted was another piece of horse meat.

"All right, just one more piece," said Henry, opening the refrigerator door. "You've stayed out of trouble for nearly two

31

weeks so I guess you deserve it."

Mrs. Huggins hung up the dish towel. Henry started to put the empty Woofies can in the step-on garbage can his mother kept under the sink. Mr. Huggins stepped aside to let Henry pull it out. Henry did not have to step on the pedal to raise the lid. The lid was already up, because the can was so full of garbage it would not close.

Ribsy came over to sniff just in case someone had thrown away a bone by mistake. Henry carefully balanced the Woofies can on top of some potato peelings. He was about to push the garbage can back under the sink when his mother spoke. "I am tired of taking out the garbage," she announced firmly.

Henry and his father looked at each other. Then Mr. Huggins said, "Henry, your mother is tired of taking out the garbage."

Henry didn't say anything. He didn't

want to get mixed up with garbage.

"I have taken out the garbage every day for eleven years," said Henry's mother.

"Eleven years," said Mr. Huggins. "Think of it!"

"Day in and day out," said Mrs. Huggins, and laughed.

"Year after year," Mr. Huggins went on.

Henry did not see why his mother and father thought this was so funny. He couldn't say he was tired of taking out the garbage, because he had never taken it out. Instead he said, "Well, so long. I'm supposed to go over to Robert's house to work on his electric train."

"Just a minute, Henry," said his father. "It's just as much your garbage as ours."

Henry didn't think this was very amusing. "Aw . . ." he muttered. He didn't want to have anything to do with smelly old garbage. None of the other kids on Klickitat Street took out garbage, at least not every day.

"I'll tell you what I'll do," said Mr. Huggins. "I'll raise your allowance fifteen cents a week if you'll take out the garbage."

"You mean take it out every day?" asked Henry, in case his father might mean every other day. He eyed the heaped-up can. Garbage, ugh! He could understand his mother's being tired of it, all right.

"Every day," said Mr. Huggins firmly.

"Maybe there's something else I could do to earn fifteen cents," Henry suggested hopefully. "Something like . . . like . . ."

"No," said his father, "just garbage."

Henry thought. His allowance was now twenty-five cents a week. That plus ten cents made thirty-five cents, plus another nickel made forty cents. He could find lots of uses for the extra money. Most fathers would just say, "Take out the garbage," without offering to pay for the job. And there probably were worse things than garbage, although right now Henry couldn't think what. Besides, if he didn't say yes, his father might tell him he had to take it out anyway.

"OK, it's a deal," said Henry without any enthusiasm. He held his nose with one hand and lifted the garbage container out of the step-on can with the other.

"Oh, it's not as bad as all that," said Mrs. Huggins cheerfully. "It's nice fresh garbage."

Ribsy followed Henry out the back door, sniffing as he went, and watched Henry lift the lid off the thirty-gallon galvanized metal can that was just like the can standing by the back door of every other house on Klickitat Street. Henry peered into the can, which was half full of garbage. Ribsy put his paws on the edge of the can and peered in, too. Most of the garbage was wrapped in newspapers so it was not as bad as Henry had expected. However, some of the juicier

garbage had soaked through the paper, and
the whole thing was pretty smelly, especially
a couple of old tuna fish cans. Henry emptied the container and took it back into the

kitchen. Then he and Ribsy went over to Robert's house.

That week Henry took out the garbage every day. His mother never had to remind him more than twice. By the end of the week the can was full of soggy newspapers, old dog food cans, pea pods, grass clippings, chicken bones which Ribsy was not allowed to chew, used tea bags, and dabs of this and that, all blended into a tangled smelly mess. Henry could not keep from peering into the can to see how awful it all was. Ugh, thought Henry, and hoped he wouldn't have to take the garbage out for eleven years. He wondered how much one of those electric garbage chopper-uppers cost that some people had installed in their sinks.

Henry had never thought much about Monday before, but now it was an important day—the day the garbage man emptied the can and hauled away the garbage. Then Henry could start all over with a new set of smells.

Monday morning Robert and Scooter came over to Henry's house to see what they could find to do. Scooter tinkered with the chain on his bicycle, Henry held one end of a rope while Ribsy tugged at the other end, and Robert sat on the front steps and thought. In the distance Henry could hear the rattle and thump of garbage cans as the garbageman emptied them.

Robert spoke first. "There was a girl in my room at school last year who was double-jointed."

"That's nothing. So am I," boasted Scooter. "See how far back I can pull my thumb."

"I can pull my thumb back farther than that," said Henry, jerking the rope to make the game of tug-of-war more interesting for Ribsy. The rattles and thumps of the garbage cans were growing louder, Henry thought, and the garbagemen must be almost at his house.

"Aw, you guys aren't really double-jointed," said Robert. "This girl in my room could bend her fingers backward without pushing them with her other hand."

The garbage truck had stopped between the Hugginses' and the Grumbies' houses. The boys watched two big men get out of the truck and balance their barrels on their shoulders. One went across the street to pick up the garbage. The other walked up the driveway between Henry's house and the house next door.

The boys forgot about double joints. "Gee, I hope I have muscles like that some-day," said Robert.

Henry did not answer. He noticed that Ribsy had dropped his end of the rope and was looking anxiously toward the back of the house. He heard the thump of the Grumbies' garbage can. The man came down the driveway with his barrel full of the Grumbies' garbage, emptied it into the truck, and walked up the driveway with the barrel once more. Ribsy watched every move he made. Then Henry heard the man take the lid off the Hugginses' can.

Ribsy growled deep in his throat. Henry

looked at him anxiously. It was the first time
he had ever heard him growl anything but a
pretend growl. Suddenly Ribsy flew into a
frenzy of barking and tore down the driveway toward the back of the house. Henry
was too shocked to move. He sat listening to
Ribsy snarl and bark. Ribsy! He couldn't

believe it—not good old Ribsy. Now he really was in trouble.

Scooter was the first to move. "Boy, is he mad about something!" he exclaimed, and ran over to the driveway.

Then Henry got into action. He started down the driveway, but what he saw made him stop. Ribsy was growling and jumping at the garbageman, who was using his empty barrel to protect himself.

"Ribsy!" wailed Henry. "Cut that out!"

Ribsy continued to snarl and advance while the garbageman retreated down the driveway behind his barrel. When Henry tried to grab Ribsy, the garbageman picked up his barrel and ran toward the truck. He threw the barrel up onto the garbage in the back of his truck and jumped inside the cab. Ribsy had his front paws on the running board before Henry could grab him by the collar.

"You keep that dog shut up or you keep

your garbage. Understand?" The garbage-man glared at Ribsy, who was still growling deep in his throat.

"But he's not really a fierce dog," protested Henry, while Ribsy strained so hard at his collar that he choked and coughed.

"Not much he isn't," said the garbage-man. "You keep him shut up when I come around. See?"

"Yes, sir." Henry knew he couldn't explain that Ribsy wasn't a fierce dog—not after the way he had just behaved.

As soon as the garbagemen drove on, Ribsy stopped growling. He looked at Henry and wagged his tail as if he expected to be praised for what he had done. Henry was too stunned to say anything for a minute. Then he said crossly, "Now look what you've done. You've got us both in trouble, that's what." Henry scowled at his dog. His father had told him he must keep Ribsy out of trouble if he wanted to go salmon fishing and now, for no reason he could see, Ribsy had attacked the garbageman. And if he had bitten the garbageman ... Well, Henry could not bring himself to think about it, because he knew that biting dogs were sent to the pound.

Scooter was careful to stay a few feet away from Ribsy. "I wouldn't get too close to him if I were you," he said. "He looks pretty ferocious."

Henry looked sadly at Ribsy, who rolled over on his back with his four feet in the air to show that he wanted his stomach scratched. "See, he isn't a bit ferocious." Henry was anxious to defend his dog, even though he knew he couldn't convince Scooter.

"You just saw him, didn't you?" asked Scooter.

"But that wasn't like Ribsy," protested Robert. "He's a good dog." Henry noticed that even though Robert defended Ribsy he was careful to stay away from him, too.

"Oh, I don't know," said Scooter. "You never can tell about dogs. Sometimes they get mean."

"Not my dog," said Henry, trying frantically to think of an explanation for Ribsy's behavior. "Maybe he just doesn't like garbagemen." That gave him a better idea. "Say, maybe the garbageman reminds Ribsy of the vet," he said excitedly. "Once when Ribsy got foxtails in his ears from running through some tall grass, we had to take him to the vet to have them taken out. The vet had to hurt Ribsy to get the foxtails out of his ears, and for a long time afterward every time I got a haircut Ribsy would sit outside the barbershop and bark at the barber because he wore a white coat like the vet."

"I suppose Ribsy thought you went to the barber to have foxtails taken out of your ears," jeered Scooter. "Besides, the garbageman doesn't wear a white coat. He wears blue overalls."

Leave it to old Scooter to spoil an explanation. "Yeah, I guess that's right," Henry answered dejectedly. How did he get mixed up in these things, anyway? He had been sitting on the front steps, just minding his own business, and now all of a sudden he was in trouble. And the worst of it was, Scooter had seen the whole thing. Now everyone on Klickitat Street would know about Ribsy.

And then Henry realized he had another problem—the garbage. A whole week's collection was still in the can in the backyard. What was worse, it was going to stay there for seven days until the garbageman came around again. What was he going to do with the garbage he had to take out until then?

That evening Henry put off telling his mother and father what had happened until they were washing dishes and he was cutting up horse meat for Ribsy.

They both looked serious. "I can't understand it," said Mrs. Huggins. "He's always been such a good-natured animal. If he really is getting to be ferocious, maybe we should keep him tied up."

"Oh, Mom, no," protested Henry. "He hates to be tied up, and anyway he always chews through the rope." Henry hoped his mother wouldn't mention buying a chain. Why, he wouldn't have any fun with Ribsy chained in the yard—not even riding his bike. It wouldn't be the same without Ribsy riding in the box tied to the back fender or loping along beside him.

"There must be some reason for his not liking the garbageman," said Mr. Huggins. "I wonder if the garbageman ever kicked him."

"Gee, Dad, do you think so?" Henry asked eagerly.

"Oh, I'm sure he wouldn't do that," said Mrs. Huggins.

Henry was anxious to change the subject before anything more was said about tying Ribsy in the backyard. He lifted the container out of the step-on garbage can and started to go out. Then, with a groan, he remembered that the can outside was already full. "Jeepers, Mom, what'll I do with the garbage?" he asked.

"You'll just have to manage the best you can. Push it down in the can somehow." Mrs. Huggins wiped a cup and sighed. "Henry, I don't know how you get mixed up in things the way you do."

Henry emptied the container on top of the garbage in the big can and tried to put the lid on again. He pushed it down as hard as he could, but it would not close. The can was extra full because Mr. Huggins had mowed the lawn again and emptied the grass clippings into it. "You old dog, you," Henry said crossly to Ribsy, who was sniffing the can. "It'll be all your fault if I don't get to go fishing."

Ribsy sat down and scratched a flea while Henry stared gloomily at the garbage can. There was one thing he was sure of. When he grew up and had a boy of his own, he would never ask him to take out the garbage.

Unfortunately, that week turned out to be unusually warm. Tuesday evening when Henry and his mother and father were eating dinner, a breeze moved the curtains at the dining-room window. "Pee-yew," said Henry, catching a whiff of overripe garbage from the can below.

"Never mind the sound effects," said Mr. Huggins, as he got up from the table to close the window. This made it very warm in the dining room.

It was even warmer in the kitchen when Henry's mother and father were washing and wiping dishes. Mrs. Huggins had to put down the dish towel several times to swat flies.

Henry fed Ribsy in silence. He dreaded the trip to the garbage can. When he could put it off no longer, he picked up the container and started out, followed closely by Ribsy. This time he arranged the day's refuse a handful at a time around the pile. Then he balanced the lid on top. The whole thing looked and smelled terrible.

On Wednesday, when Henry walked reluctantly down the back steps with the garbage, he saw Mr. Grumbie standing on his back porch.

As Henry took the lid off the can, Mr. Grumbie looked across the driveway. "So that's where the smell is coming from," he said.

"I'm afraid it is, Mr. Grumbie," answered Henry.

"I heard about Ribsy tearing the seat out of the garbageman's overalls," said Mr. Grumbie.

Jeepers, thought Henry miserably, the story's not only going around the neighborhood, it's getting worse than it really was. Next thing, people would be saying Ribsy bit the garbageman. He explained what had really happened, and then Mr. Grumbie went in and closed all the windows that faced the Hugginses' house.

Henry grew more and more discouraged. On Thursday, after he had piled the garbage on top of the can and replaced the lid as well as he could, he got an apple box out of the garage, climbed up on it, and stepped carefully onto the lid. He stamped his feet a few times to work the garbage down into the can and then jumped up and down. It helped some but not much.

On Friday Henry suggested to his mother that they buy a second garbage can, but she did not think this was a good idea. Then Henry decided to take the garbage out before dinner when the container was not so full. He distributed the milk cartons and carrot tops as well as he could on the heap and was jumping up and down on the lid when Robert and Scooter came up the driveway looking for him.

"What are you doing up there?" Robert demanded, with one eye on Ribsy. "Look at it, Scooter! Did you ever see so much garbage?"

"Pee-yew," said Scooter, staying on the driveway well away from Ribsy, who was rolling on the grass to scratch his back.

"Never mind the sound effects." Henry jumped to the ground. It was all right for him to criticize his own garbage, but he didn't want anyone else to do it. "Come on, let's go out in front."

"Yes, let's," agreed Scooter. "Pee-yew."

Henry was about to suggest they all go over to the park. Then he decided he had better not take a chance on Ribsy's behavior toward strangers. "Come on, let's see who can walk farthest on his hands," he said, to keep Scooter and Robert from talking about his troubles.

While the three boys were busy trying to walk across the lawn on their hands, they heard a sudden clatter and crash from the backyard and promptly got on their feet.

"Sounds like a garbage can to me," said Scooter.

Henry, who had known instantly what made the noise, was already on his way around the house with Ribsy at his heels. Scooter and Robert were close behind. Henry found the garbage can tipped on its side. The lid had rolled halfway across the backyard, and garbage was strewn all the way from the steps to the cherry tree. In the midst of the litter stood a collie and another big dog. A crust of bread hung from the collie's mouth.

The dogs started to run when they saw the boys. Ribsy chased them while Henry grabbed an old Woofies can and threw it after them. "You beat it," he yelled. Then he looked at the mess and groaned. Garbage! He was sick and tired of it. He kicked at an eggshell and groaned again. It wasn't worth fifteen cents a week. It wasn't worth a hundred, or a thousand, or even a million dollars.

Scooter and Robert held their noses. Then Scooter made a gagging noise and Robert copied him.

"Aw, hey, fellows, cut it out." Henry glared at his friends and pulled the can, still half full, upright. He looked around and sighed.

"Well, I guess I better be going," said Scooter. "I just remembered I'm supposed to go to the store for my mother."

"Me, too," said Robert. "So long, Henry."

Some friends, thought Henry, and set to work. He was busy scooping up coffee grounds and mildewed pea pods when he heard his father's car turn into the driveway.

Mr. Huggins looked around the back yard. "Dogs?" he asked.

"That collie and that other big dog down the street," answered Henry.

Mr. Huggins did not say anything. He found a shovel in the garage and went to work.

"Uh . . . Dad," began Henry. "The garbageman isn't exactly a *neighbor*. Does his complaining about Ribsy mean I don't get to go fishing with you?"

"We'll see what happens Monday before we decide," answered his father. "Perhaps we can find out what made him act the way he did."

On Saturday Henry did not take the garbage out at all. When neither his mother nor his father reminded him, he guessed they must be as tired of garbage as he was.

Sunday afternoon Robert and Scooter came over to see if anything new had happened to the garbage or to Ribsy.

"Aw, fellows, forget it," said Henry. Then he saw Beezus and her little sister Ramona coming down the street. Beezus's real name was Beatrice, but Ramona called her Beezus and everyone else did, too. "Hi!" Henry was glad to be interrupted.

"Hello, Henry. Did the garbageman ever take away your garbage?" Beezus asked.

"He'll take it tomorrow," said Henry coldly. The way things got around on Klickitat Street!

"Ramona, look out!" screamed Beezus. She rushed over to her little sister, who had a firm hold on Ribsy's tail and was pulling as hard as she could. "He bites!" said Beezus. "He bit the garbageman."

"He did *not* bite the garbageman!" yelled
Henry. "Don't you dare say he did!"

Ribsy looked around at Ramona. "Wuf,"
he said mildly, and waited patiently while

Beezus frantically pried Ramona's fingers loose from his tail.

"He didn't bite when Ramona pulled his tail, did he?" Henry asked angrily.

"No." Beezus looked doubtfully at Ribsy. "But somebody told Mother he bit the garbageman."

"Oh, for Pete's sake!" Henry was thoroughly disgusted. This was too much.

"Of course, you don't know what Ribsy would have done if he had got at the garbageman," observed Scooter.

"You keep quiet." Henry glared at Scooter. "The garbageman must have kicked him or something. Look at him. Does he look the least bit cross?"

Beezus and the boys looked at Ribsy, who lay on the grass with a patient look on his face. Ramona was sitting on him. When she grabbed his ear, Ribsy looked at Henry as if to say, "Get her off me, won't you?"

"No, he doesn't look a bit cross," admitted Beezus, pulling her little sister away. "He seems to understand she's little and doesn't know any better."

Thinking secretly that Ramona did know better, Henry turned to Scooter. "Now are you satisfied?" he demanded.

"Well . . ." Scooter was not easy to satisfy.

Henry tried to think of something, anything, to change the subject. "Say, Scooter," he said, "I wish you'd take a look at the horn on my bike. It's been sounding funny lately."

"Sure," said Scooter eagerly. If there was one thing he enjoyed, it was tinkering with a bicycle. "Where is it?"

"In the garage," answered Henry, and they all started down the driveway toward the open garage doors.

As Scooter took hold of the handlebars and started to wheel the bicycle out of the garage, Ribsy began to growl deep in his throat. The hair stood up on his neck and he moved toward Scooter.

Everyone stared at Ribsy. Scooter hastily dropped the bicycle on the driveway, and Ribsy stopped growling at once. He went to Henry and wagged his tail, waiting to be praised.

"Hey, did you see that?" Henry shouted.

"I sure did," said Scooter. "He's a vicious dog!"

"He is not vicious. He was protecting my bike!" Henry was growing more excited. "He isn't cross at all. He was just protecting my bike."

Scooter did not look convinced. "Don't you see?" Henry went on. "That explains about the garbageman. Ribsy was protecting the garbage from the garbageman because he thought it was mine!"

"He's a watchdog," agreed Beezus.

"Sure," said Henry eagerly. "It takes a

smart dog to be a watchdog."

At this Robert and Scooter began to shout with laughter. "What a watchdog!" hooted Scooter.

"Whoever heard of a dog guarding the garbage?" Robert doubled up with laughter.

"Your *valuable* garbage," shouted Scooter.

"Your *precious* garbage," howled Robert.

"Aw, cut it out," said Henry sheepishly and began to laugh, partly because he thought it was funny but mostly from relief at proving that Ribsy was not a vicious dog. His fishing trip was still safe!

Robert and Scooter whooped and pounded each other on the back. Ribsy, sensing that they were laughing at him, hung his head and slunk over to Henry, who hugged him and went on laughing.

"Boy, oh, boy," gasped Scooter. "I can just see the Hugginses' backyard a year from now when it's ten feet deep—"

"In Henry's very own valuable precious garbage," finished Robert, and the boys whooped some more.

Henry stopped laughing. The picture of his backyard ten feet deep in garbage was too terrible to think about.

Mr. Huggins appeared in the kitchen door. "What's all this about?" he asked, as he joined the group on the driveway. When he heard the story, he laughed, too. He snapped his fingers at Ribsy and when the dog bounded over to him, he slapped his side and said, "You're a pretty good dog, aren't you?" Ribsy wriggled with delight.

Henry's friends, knowing it must be nearly dinnertime, started to leave. "I'll look at your horn tomorrow if you'll get your bike out of the garage yourself," promised Scooter.

"Take good care of your garbage," said Robert.

"Aw, keep quiet," answered Henry, and grinned. When the others were gone he turned to his father. "Say, Dad, about this garbage . . ."

"What about it?" asked his father.

"Well, we didn't have any trouble with Ribsy protecting it from the garbage man when Mom took it out and I was wondering . . ." Henry paused and looked at his father.

Mr. Huggins smiled. "Wondering what?"

"Well, I was wondering if there wasn't something else you would rather have me do for the extra fifteen cents than take out the garbage."

Mr. Huggins thought it over. "All right," he said, "I'll take out the garbage if you'll clip around the edge of the lawn after I mow it each week."

It was Henry's turn to think it over. Clipping the edge of the lawn was harder than taking out the garbage. It meant crawling around on his hands and knees for about an hour. Still, as far as Henry knew now, there was no possible way either he or Ribsy could get into trouble doing it. "OK, Dad," he said. "It's a deal!"

"OK," said Mr. Huggins. "But just to make sure, we'd better put Ribsy in the basement when we hear the garbageman coming."

"He won't mind for a little while," said Henry, giving the garbage can a good hard whack as he and his father went into the house.

3

Henry Gets a Haircut

Henry was looking through the refrigerator for something to eat, something that wasn't too hard and wasn't too chewy, because he had two teeth so loose he could wiggle them with his tongue. They were upper teeth, one on either side of his four grown-up front teeth. Henry wanted to keep them three more days, so he would have something to show off to the other boys the first day of school.

Ribsy pawed at the refrigerator door. "All right," said Henry, "you've been pretty good about keeping out of trouble lately." He tossed a piece of horse meat to him.

Let's see, thought Henry, poking first his loose right tooth and then his loose left tooth with his tongue, peanut butter is too sticky. I guess I'll have some bread and apricot–pineapple jam.

As he reached for the jam jar, Henry heard his mother come in the front door. "Hi, Mom," he called.

"Hi," she answered, and entered the kitchen with her arms full of packages. "Wait till you see what I bought."

"What?" asked Henry. He wiggled first his right tooth and then his left tooth as he took a slice of bread out of the bread box.

Mrs. Huggins dumped her packages on the draining board. "Electric clippers," she announced. "The Colossal Drugstore was having a sale. Only six dollars and ninety-five cents, marked down from nine ninety-five."

"Clippers for what?" Henry asked, as he spread butter on the bread. He wiggled his left tooth. Hm-m, he thought, it's a little bit looser than the right tooth.

"Hair clippers, of course," answered his mother.

Henry stopped wiggling his teeth. "Clippers for whose hair?" he asked suspiciously.

"Now, Henry," said Mrs. Huggins soothingly, "I'm sure that with a little practice I can do just as good a job as the barber. And with the price of haircuts, think of the money we'll save."

"Mom!" wailed Henry, clutching his hair. He didn't want to save money. He wanted to save his hair. "Are you going to cut Dad's hair, too?"

Mrs. Huggins laughed as she unwrapped the clippers. "Your father's hair is precious, now that it's getting so thin on top. We can't afford to take chances with it."

"My hair's precious, too," said Henry, deciding he wasn't hungry after all. He handed Ribsy the bread and butter and watched him gulp it down. Then he leaned gloomily against the refrigerator and wiggled first his right tooth and then his left tooth. Jeepers, he thought, now what am I going to do?

Mrs. Huggins took a sheet out of a drawer. "Henry, why do you keep making such awful faces?" she asked.

"I'm not making faces," said Henry. "I'm wiggling my loose teeth."

"Which teeth are loose?" Mrs. Huggins asked.

Maybe she'll forget about cutting my hair, thought Henry, as he went to his mother and bared his teeth. "Thee, thith and thith," he lisped, as he wiggled first his right tooth and then his left tooth with his tongue.

"They're your canine teeth," remarked Mrs. Huggins.

"Canine?" repeated Henry, delighted that he was distracting his mother. "I thought canine meant dog."

"It does," answered his mother. "The cuspids are called canine teeth, because they're pointed like a dog's teeth."

"Hey, teeth like a dog," said Henry. He bared his teeth and growled at Ribsy.

Then Mrs. Huggins said briskly, "Now, Henry, don't try to change the subject. You sit on this chair and put this sheet around your neck and I'll go to work."

"Right this minute?" Henry asked mournfully.

"Right this minute," said Mrs. Huggins. "Your hair is so scraggly on the back of your neck it looks like fringe."

"Mom," wailed Henry, "you can't do this to me."

"Now, Henry, don't worry," said his mother reassuringly. "On the way home I stopped and watched a barber cutting hair, so I know just how it's done."

"Do you think Dad will want you to cut my hair?" Henry asked.

"Oh, yes," answered Mrs. Huggins. "I phoned him and talked it over with him before I bought the clippers. He thought it was a good idea."

I might have known they'd stick together, Henry thought miserably, as he slid down in the chair. Why can't the phone ring or something?

Mrs. Huggins plugged the clippers into the wall and turned on the switch. They chattered so furiously that Henry could not help ducking. Ribsy tucked his tail between

his legs and hastily left the kitchen.

Henry felt his mother's hand on top of his head and heard the clippers at the back of his neck. Then he felt them touch his skin. "Ow," he exclaimed, and pulled away. "They're cold."

"Now, Henry, I haven't even begun to clip," said his mother.

Henry gritted his teeth. The clippers touched the back of his neck and whizzed up his head. "Mom!" protested Henry, feeling the back of his head. "That's too short."

"The clippers do cut awfully fast." For the first time Mrs. Huggins sounded doubtful.

Once more the clippers tickled Henry's neck and chattered up the back of his head. "There," said Mrs. Huggins. "I didn't get it quite so close that time."

"But it's supposed to match," said Henry.

"I'll take a little off right here to even it up," said Mrs. Huggins.

The clippers swooped down on Henry's head. Then they whizzed up the back again. Just wait till the kids see this, thought Henry gloomily.

"Hey, what's going on in here?" It was Henry's father. The clippers made so much noise that neither Henry nor his mother had heard him come in.

"Dad," wailed Henry, "look what Mom's done to me."

"Hm-m," said Mr. Huggins, "your hair looks as if the moths had got into it."

Mrs. Huggins began to laugh, but Henry did not think it was very funny. Who wanted to go around with moth-eaten hair? He slid farther down in his chair and scowled at the kitchen wall.

"Here, let me try," said Mr. Huggins. "I ought to know how to cut hair. I've watched the barber cut mine often enough." He started the clippers chattering again.

Henry sat up. Maybe his father would be better at cutting hair. He felt his right ear being folded down and heard the clippers whiz up the side of his head.

"Oops!" said Mr. Huggins.

"What do you mean, oops?" demanded Henry crossly.

Instead of answering, Mr. Huggins put his hand under Henry's chin, tipped his head back, and looked first at the right side and then at the left. He folded down Henry's left ear and ran the clippers up the side of his head. Then he stepped back to look at the results. "Not too bad," he observed.

Henry groaned.

"What'll we do with the top?" asked Henry's father. "Mow it?"

"Dad!" yelled Henry.

Mrs. Huggins giggled. Henry scowled.

Mr. Huggins held a lock of Henry's hair up with a comb and sheared the ends off with the clippers. "This isn't so easy," he said. "Your hair grows every which way back here." He combed and clipped another lock and then another. "There," he said at last, and turned off the clippers.

Neither of Henry's parents spoke.

"Let me see." Henry jerked off the sheet and ran to the mirror in his room. He stared, too horrified to speak. His hair was shorter on the left side than on the right. Both sides were rough and the top looked chewed. Henry ran his hands over the back of his head. He did not need to see it. He could tell what his father meant about moths. He could never go outdoors looking like this. He would have to stay in the house for weeks, even months, until his hair grew out.

Mrs. Huggins came into the room and put her arm around Henry's shoulders. "I'm sorry, Henry. I thought I could do a better job," she said. "I'm sure it will look all right in a few days."

"Don't worry, son," said Mr. Huggins.

"It'll grow out in no time and next time we'll do better."

"Next time!" Henry stared at himself in the mirror. "I can't go to school looking like this. I'll have to stay home. I'll get behind in arithmetic and I won't know the folk dances and—"

"Oh, Henry," interrupted his mother, "it isn't that bad. It will be grown out before you know it."

"But it won't grow out by Monday and that's when school starts."

When Henry's mother and father left the room, Henry threw himself on the bed and pounded the pillow with his fist. He would have to think of something to do about his hair. He would just have to, that was all. Maybe he could get a wig. Or have all his hair cut off and say he was tired of having hair. There was one thing he was sure of. He couldn't face the kids, especially Scooter, looking like this. Some bits of hair that had fallen down Henry's back made him itch. He scratched and thought.

Then he got up and pulled his Daniel Boone coonskin hat out of a drawer. He put it on and looked at himself in the mirror. No, it wouldn't do. Even with the tail hanging down, too much hair showed. He put it back and pulled out his sailor hat. No, it wouldn't do either. Wait a minute, he thought, and turned down the brim. Yes, that did it. The turned down brim hid every bit of his hair. It hid his eyebrows, too, but he didn't care.

Henry looked at himself in the mirror, wiggled first his right tooth and then his left tooth, and felt a little better. Maybe he could find something to rub into his scalp to stimulate the growth of hair the way the advertisements said.

Ribsy whimpered at the front door.

Henry let him out and then decided to go out with him. Even if he did look funny, he'd better keep his eye on Ribsy every minute. He wasn't going to miss that fishing trip if he could help it.

Henry sat on the front steps with his arm around Ribsy's neck and laid his cheek against Ribsy's ear. Good old Ribsy. He seemed to understand. Funny how Ribsy's ears were so silky when the rest of his hair was so rough. And he smelled good, too—a nice doggy smell. Henry scratched Ribsy behind his right ear. Thump, thump, thump went Ribsy's tail on the step.

Then Ribsy trotted into the shrubbery and came back with his rope, which he dropped at Henry's feet. He looked at Henry and wagged his tail.

"Oh, so you want to play tug-of-war." Henry tossed one end of the rope to his dog, who grabbed it with his mouth and growled a pretend growl. Henry pulled at the rope. Ribsy hung on and pulled harder. "Good old Ribsy," said Henry. It wasn't every dog that would play tug-of-war.

Henry was still playing with Ribsy when he noticed Scooter McCarthy pedaling down Klickitat Street on his bicycle with Robert riding on the back fender. It was too late for Henry to retreat into the house. His friends had already seen him.

Scooter stopped in front of Henry. "Hi," he said. "What are you wearing that sailor hat like that for?"

"None of your beeswax," answered Henry.

The two boys got off the bicycle and joined Henry on the steps. Henry watched Scooter in case he tried to snatch the sailor hat.

"I bet all your hair fell out," said Scooter. "I bet you're bald."

"My hair didn't either fall out," said Henry.

"Then why—" began Robert.

Henry quickly interrupted. "I have two loose teeth," he said to change the subject. "Thee, thith and thith. They're canine teeth. That means teeth like a dog."

"Aw, I lost those teeth ages ago," boasted Scooter.

"Sure you did," said Henry. "You're older than me."

"How about letting me pull them for you?" suggested Scooter.

"No, let me," begged Robert.

"Nope," said Henry, pleased at getting their attention away from his hat.

"Aw, come on, Huggins," coaxed Scooter. "I'll give you a piece of Chinese money that has a hole in the center."

Henry shook his head. He hoped he could keep them talking about his teeth

until his mother called him in to dinner.

"Please, Henry," said Robert. "I'll let you make a tunnel out of a coffee can for my electric railroad."

Henry did not answer. He wiggled his teeth and kept an eye on Scooter.

"You keep quiet," Scooter said to Robert. "I asked him first."

"He's more my friend than he is yours," answered Robert. "We're the same age and we're in the same room at school."

Henry wiggled his teeth and let the boys argue. While they were arguing, Mary Jane, Beezus, and her little sister Ramona came down the street. Henry could tell they had been to the store, because Mary Jane was carrying a jar of mayonnaise, Beezus a carton of milk, and Ramona a pound of butter, which wouldn't break if she dropped it.

"Henry has two loose teeth at the same time," Robert announced to the girls.

"Let's see," said Beezus eagerly.

"Oh, it's nothing," said Henry modestly, and bared his teeth. He wiggled first the right tooth and then the left tooth while the girls watched and admired. If he kept them busy looking at his teeth, they might not say anything about his hat.

"If you'll tie strings to them, I'll be glad to pull them for you," said Beezus.

"Hey, I asked first," Scooter reminded Henry.

"Nope," said Henry.

"Henry Huggins, you better pull them out," said Mary Jane. "My dentist says if you leave loose teeth in too long it makes your grown-up teeth come in crooked."

Henry scratched at the bits of hair down his back as he thought this over. "Nope," he said, to keep the argument going, "I'm going to keep them."

"If you tie strings on them and tie the other ends to a doorknob and slam the door, they come out without even hurting," said Beezus.

"He could eat a whole bunch of chewy

candy. That would pull the teeth out," suggested Mary Jane.

"That's no fun," objected Scooter. "Besides, he might swallow them."

"He could tie a string to each tooth and then tie rocks to the other ends of the strings and throw the rocks in the river." Robert looked pleased with his suggestion.

"I know a better way," said Scooter. "He could tie the rocks to his teeth and walk along a railroad track until he came to a high trestle, and when he got to the middle he could throw the rocks off. Boy, that would really pull them out!"

"I know," said Robert. "He could tie the other ends of the strings to the back end of a fire engine, and when it took off—yow! Would his teeth come out in a hurry!"

"He could tie them to a skyrocket and set off the rocket. Zowie! That would really be something to watch." Scooter looked proud of himself for thinking up this idea.

"Now you're being silly," said Mary Jane. "Anyway, the Fourth of July is past."

"Say, whose teeth are they, anyway?" demanded Henry. Was Scooter eyeing his hat? He couldn't be sure, so he continued. "Besides, I don't want to lose the teeth for keeps. I want to put them under my pillow at night and find dimes instead of teeth in the morning. Anyway, I'll think of a way to pull them myself."

"How?" everyone wanted to know.

"You just wait," said Henry. "It'll be a good way, a way nobody ever pulled teeth before." Then he wished he hadn't said it. Now he would have to think of a way to pull the teeth, and he already had enough troubles. He scratched his back where the loose hair made him itch and wished his mother would hurry up and call him in to dinner.

"What do you keep scratching for?" Scooter asked, glancing at Henry's hat.

"I itch," said Henry coldly.

"Ramona!" shrieked Beezus suddenly. "Now look what you've done!"

Ramona was busy eating the pound of butter, which she had unwrapped and was holding in her grimy little hands. Ribsy finished licking the greasy paper and moved closer to help Ramona finish the butter.

"Ribsy!" yelled Henry, and grabbed his dog by the collar. He couldn't have Ribsy eating the Quimbys' butter. Beezus's mother would be sure to complain if he did. The Quimbys might eat butter that had been licked by Ramona, but they probably wouldn't eat butter licked by Ribsy even though he was a nice clean dog.

Ribsy strained so hard toward the butter that Henry had to hang onto his collar with both hands. Ribsy coughed and pawed the

air with his front feet. "Cut it out, Ribsy,"
ordered Henry. "Do you want to get me in
trouble?"

"Ramona, just wait till Mother sees this
butter," scolded Beezus, as she pried at her

little sister's slippery fingers. "Look at it. It's all squeezed and dirty."

Out of the corner of his eye Henry saw Scooter raise his hand. Henry let go of Ribsy's collar, the dog bounded forward, and Henry clapped his hands to his head an instant too late. Scooter had snatched the sailor hat.

"You give me that hat!" yelled Henry, trying to cover his hair with one hand while he grabbed at his hat with the other.

"Try and get it," taunted Scooter, and began to laugh. "Boy, oh, boy! Look at the haircut!"

"Ribsy!" screamed Beezus.

"I've got him," said Robert, grabbing Ribsy by the collar.

"Henry Huggins, what happened to you?" Mary Jane was horrified. "You look all chewed."

"Wow!" exclaimed Robert, keeping a firm grip on Ribsy's collar. "Look at that hair!"

"Scooter McCarthy, you give me that hat!" Henry tried to grab it, but Scooter held it out of reach.

"What happened, Henry?" Robert asked. "Did you cut your own hair?"

"Aw, keep quiet," said Henry.

"It looks as if something had been chewing on it!" Scooter stopped and laughed. "Look at it. Did you ever see anything so chewed?"

Beezus, who was trying to stuff the melting remains of the butter back into the box, looked at Henry. "I know what happened. His mother cut his hair, that's what. I can tell, because my mother cuts my hair and she never gets the bangs straight."

"Is that what happened?" Scooter demanded, as he spun Henry's hat around on his finger.

Henry kicked at a tuft of grass. He was too miserable to answer.

"Boy, she really fixed you," said Scooter,

laughing harder than ever. "Look at those nicks in back. And the way it sticks out over your ears."

"I'm glad my mother doesn't cut my hair," said Robert. "I wouldn't want to go around looking like that."

"Wait till the kids at school see it," said Scooter. "I wouldn't want to be in your shoes."

"It does look pretty awful," said Beezus, as she tried to hang onto her little sister's greasy fingers. "I guess it's easier to cut girls' hair."

Henry did not have a thing to say. He knew how awful his hair looked.

At last Mrs. Huggins came out on the porch. "Henry, dinner is ready," she called.

Henry caught the sailor hat as Scooter tossed it to him. "Come on, you old dog," he said to Ribsy as he climbed the front steps. "Look at all the trouble you got me into just because I was trying to keep you out of trouble. Now what am I going to do?"

Ribsy's ears and tail drooped as he followed Henry into the house.

4

Henry's Canine Teeth

That evening, when Henry wore his sailor hat to the dinner table, he noticed his mother glance at him and then look at his father. She looked as if she was going to say something, but instead she sighed and was silent.

"You're looking pretty gloomy," remarked Mr. Huggins, as he filled Henry's plate.

"Yeah," said Henry. "Don't give me much to eat. I'm not very hungry." Henry was careful to bite with his solid front teeth. He couldn't take chances with his loose teeth. He had to have them to show off to people who started making fun of his hair.

"I'm afraid the boys were giving him a bad time about his hair," exclaimed Mrs. Huggins.

"Would you feel better if you went to the barber to see what he could do about it?" asked Henry's father. "A short crew cut might help."

"Well, maybe, but I don't think anything would help very much," said Henry. He wiggled first his right tooth and then his left tooth.

"I wonder if . . ." began Mrs. Huggins and paused.

"If what?" Mr. Huggins asked.

"Oh, nothing. I was just thinking." Mrs.

Huggins suddenly smiled at Henry.

Henry wiggled his teeth and wondered what his mother was thinking about. He hoped it wasn't anything like another home haircut.

"Really, Henry," said his mother, "you shouldn't go around with your teeth flapping that way."

"Aw, Mom, they don't flap," protested Henry. "They just wiggle."

"I see by the paper that old teeth left under pillows are turning into quarters instead of dimes, because the cost of living has gone up," said Mr. Huggins.

Henry grinned. He knew it was really his father who had always taken away his old teeth and left the dimes under his pillow. But right now, much as he could use two quarters, he needed two loose teeth more.

The next morning Henry examined his hair in the mirror. He could not see that it had grown any, so he put on his sailor hat and moped around the house. He tried drawing a face on an electric lightbulb with colored chalk. When he found the face did not shine through the shade the way he had planned, he felt even gloomier. He stood with his nose pressed against the front windowpane until Ribsy scratched at the door and asked to be let out.

Henry followed his dog out the door and sat down on the front steps. Gloomy as he felt about his hair, he didn't want to risk losing that fishing trip by giving Ribsy a chance to get into trouble with the neighbors. While he kept his eye on Ribsy, he could not keep from poking first his right tooth and then his left tooth with his tongue. They were looser all right. He discovered he could poke the two teeth out between his lips so they felt like little tusks.

As Henry experimented with his teeth,

he happened to glance up Klickitat Street. Then, thinking he must be seeing things, he jumped up and stared. Robert and Scooter were walking toward him, both of them wearing sailor hats with the brims turned down over their eyebrows!

Well, how do you like that, thought Henry. Wearing sailor hats just to make fun of me. A couple of fine friends they turned out to be. Well, they weren't going to get a chance to tease him. "Come on, Ribsy," he said. "Let's go in the house before they see us."

Ribsy did not care to go into the house. He was busy sniffing the rosebushes along the edge of the Grumbies' property.

"OK, you old dog," muttered Henry, and steeled himself for the meeting with Scooter and Robert.

Side by side the two boys walked down the street. They did not seem to see Henry.

Looking straight ahead, they stalked past the Hugginses' house.

Henry stared after them. What's the matter with them anyhow? he wondered. What did I do to them? Then a thought struck Henry. Could it be? No, it couldn't.

Yes, it must be! Suddenly Henry had a feeling he was no longer the only boy with a chewed-up haircut. "Hey!" he yelled.

Robert and Scooter stalked on.

Why are they acting like that, Henry wondered. It's not my fault if they have home haircuts. Henry felt he had to know for sure. If he wasn't the only one with chewed-up hair, things wouldn't be so bad. "Hey, fellows," he yelled again and as he yelled, his tongue touched one of his loose teeth. What were a couple of loose teeth anyhow? He made up his mind. "Want to watch me pull my teeth?"

Robert and Scooter hesitated. Then they stopped and turned around.

"I've thought of a keen way to pull them," said Henry, trying frantically to think of an unusual way to get those teeth out of his mouth.

"How?" demanded Scooter, as he and

Robert came up to the steps.

"You'll see," said Henry feebly. But, he thought, how *am* I going to pull them? To stall for time, he fished through his pockets and found a piece of string. "Uh . . . how come you fellows are wearing hats?" he ventured.

"Come on, Robert," said Scooter. "He said he was going to pull his teeth, but I guess he didn't mean it."

"I am too going to pull them." Henry was determined not to let the boys get away before he found out what had happened. He carefully untangled the string and tried to sound casual. "Did you fellows get your hair cut?" he asked.

"We sure did," said Scooter, "and it's all your fault."

"What do you mean, it's all my fault?" asked Henry. "What did I do?"

"You know." Scooter scowled at Henry.

"And if you ask me it was a pretty mean trick. As bad as tattling."

"Worse," said Robert.

"What mean trick?" Henry demanded. "What are you talking about?"

"Your mother phoned our mothers and told them about the sale of hair clippers, that's what," said Scooter. "She phoned just like you told her to. And they both went right over to the clipper sale at the Colossal Drugstore."

"My mother?" Henry was genuinely bewildered. "My mother phoned your mothers?"

"Honest, didn't you know about it?" Robert asked.

"Cross my heart and hope to die," said Henry. Well, so that was what his mother had been thinking about at dinner last night! Leave it to her to think of something. Henry wanted to laugh and shout but he didn't dare, not with Scooter glowering at him.

"See?" said Robert to Scooter. "I told you it wasn't his idea for his mother to tell our mothers. I knew Henry wouldn't do a thing like that and you said he would."

Henry looked injured. "You're some friend, thinking I'd do a mean thing like that."

"Well, maybe you didn't," said Scooter grudgingly, "but I bet you haven't really thought of a way to pull your teeth."

"I have, too," said Henry. Now how was he going to get out of this fix, he wondered, as he slowly tied one end of the string to his right tooth. Then he slowly tied the other end of the string to his left tooth while he tried to think of a way to stall for time. "How about letting me have a look at your hair?" he suggested, anxious to see if their haircuts were worse than his.

"Come on! Let's see you pull your teeth," said Scooter.

"I need some more string," explained Henry. "I can't pull them until somebody gives me some more string."

Robert and Scooter searched their pockets. "I don't have any," said Robert.

"Me neither," said Scooter. "You're just stalling."

"I'm not either stalling." Should he suggest they go around to the backyard, Henry wondered. Maybe he could climb the cherry tree and hang the string that joined his two teeth over a branch and jump out of the tree. It was not much of an idea, but it would have to do.

Henry started to call Ribsy, who was napping with his nose on his paws, when suddenly he had an inspiration. Of course! Why hadn't he thought of it before! All he needed was a little cooperation from Ribsy, and this time he had a feeling that for once Ribsy would do the right thing at the right time.

Henry picked up Ribsy's tug-of-war rope. He tied one end to the middle of the string that joined his two teeth and tossed the other end onto the grass. "Here, Ribsy," he called. Ribsy opened one eye and looked at Henry. Then he opened the other eye and bounded across the lawn. "Wuf!" he said.

Henry braced himself in case it hurt to have his teeth pulled. Ribsy grabbed the end of the rope, growled deep in his throat, and tugged. Henry's teeth flew out of his mouth so fast he didn't even feel them go.

Henry put his hand to his mouth and stared at his teeth lying on the grass. They had come out so easily he could scarcely believe they were gone. He poked his tongue into the right hole in his mouth and then into the left hole. They were gone, all right. "How's that for a way to pull teeth?" he asked. "They were canine teeth, so I thought I'd let my dog pull them out."

"Say, that was a smart idea," exclaimed Robert. "I never heard of anyone having a dog pull his teeth before. Maybe I can get him to pull the next one I have loose."

"Good old Ribsy," said Henry, and hugged him. Maybe Ribsy did get into a little trouble once in a while, but he was

pretty useful for getting out of a tight spot.
Ribsy wriggled with delight and licked
Henry's face with his long pink tongue.

"A tooth-pulling dog. That's pretty
good." Scooter sounded impressed. "Take
you long to train the old garbage hound?"

"Not very long, and he's *not* a garbage

hound." Henry untied his teeth and put them in the watch pocket of his jeans for safekeeping till he put them under his pillow that night. "He's a smart dog, aren't you, Ribsy?"

"Wuf," answered Ribsy, and worried the rope.

Henry looked at Scooter's and Robert's sailor hats. "Well, how about letting me see your haircuts?" he asked, pulling off his own hat.

"Nope." Scooter took hold of his hat and tried to yank it farther down over his ears.

"Aw, come on, Scoot," coaxed Henry. "I pulled my teeth like I said I would."

Robert snatched off his own hat, and he and Henry studied each other's haircuts. "Yours is better in front but mine is better in back," Robert decided. "At least it feels better."

Henry examined Robert's hair. It looked

pretty bad, a little worse than his own he decided, especially where it was gouged out over the left ear. "I suppose hair really does grow pretty fast," said Henry.

"Anyway, we're better off than Scooter," observed Robert. "He's bald on one side. It'll take months to grow out."

"No kidding?" said Henry. "Really bald?" Then he and Robert began to laugh.

Scooter looked even gloomier. "It's all right for you guys to laugh. You're in the same room at school and you can stick together, but I'll be the only one in my room who doesn't have a boughten haircut."

"Gee, that's tough," said Robert, but he didn't sound very sorry.

"It sure is," agreed Henry cheerfully. What did he care about his haircut? As Scooter said, he and Robert could stick together.

Then Henry had an idea. "Hey, fellows, look!" he said. He turned on the garden hose, filled his mouth with water and blew as hard as he could. Two streams of water shot through the gaps in his teeth. "I bet you wish you could spit double," he said. Boy, oh, boy! He still had something to show the kids at school. Something besides his haircut.

5
Ramona and the P.T.A.

Henry Huggins and Scooter McCarthy were riding home on their bicycles one day after school early in September. Ribsy, who always waited for Henry under the fir tree in the schoolyard, was riding in the box Henry had tied to the back fender of his bicycle.

"You going salmon fishing this week-end?" asked Scooter, steering his bicycle through a pile of autumn leaves in the gutter.

"I don't know. Dad hasn't said anything about it," answered Henry.

"My dad took me down on the Umptucca River last Saturday," said Scooter.

"Catch anything?" asked Henry, trying to keep his excitement out of his voice. If salmon were biting on the Umptucca, maybe his father would go fishing next Saturday.

"Well, I didn't exactly catch anything," said Scooter.

"How do you mean, not exactly?" Henry asked.

"I thought I had a bite once, but I didn't exactly land the fish," said Scooter. "But I bet I get one the next time."

The two boys pedaled along Klickitat Street. Henry was hoping his father would go fishing on Saturday. He would almost surely get to go, because he had kept Ribsy out of trouble—at least the kind of trouble the neighbors might complain about. Of course there had been a couple of close calls, but Henry had lived up to his side of the bargain and now he had nothing to worry about.

"So long," called Scooter, when the boys came to the Hugginses' house.

"So long." Henry rode up the driveway and parked his bicycle in the garage. The back door was locked, so he found the key under the door mat and let himself in. Beside the refrigerator he found a note from his mother that said, "Have gone to P.T.A. meeting. Don't eat all the wienies. Mother."

Henry took two wienies, which he shared with Ribsy. While Henry was eating his wienie and thinking about catching a salmon, the doorbell rang.

When Henry went to the door, he found

Beezus and her little sister Ramona standing on the front porch licking ice cream cones. Ramona, who carried a square blue lunch box in one hand, was having trouble managing her cone with the other. Her chin and the bib of her overalls were smeared with chocolate ice cream.

"Hello, Henry," said Beezus. "Can you come over to my house and play checkers?"

"Sure, that's a keen idea," answered Henry. "I bet I can beat you." Checkers was one of his favorite games and Beezus was a good player. She didn't take all day to make a move the way some girls did.

Ribsy looked hungrily at the ice cream cones. He knew Henry always saved the last bite of a cone for him. Maybe the girls would give him a bite, too. Ribsy swallowed and wagged his tail.

"Go away," Henry said to him. "You can't have any of their ice cream." Ribsy made a whimpering noise.

"What's Ramona carrying a lunch box for?" Henry asked. "She doesn't go to school."

"It's not a lunch box," said Ramona, as a little river of ice cream dribbled off her chin.

"It is too a lunch box," said Henry.

Beezus ran her tongue all the way around her ice-cream cone. "Ramona's pretending it's a camera," she explained.

"How can she pretend a lunch box is a camera?" Henry wanted to know. A lunch box for a camera! What a dumb idea!

"Oh, she has lots of imagination," said Beezus. "Daddy says she has too much."

"I'm going to take your picture," announced Ramona. She held one end of the lunch box against her stomach. The other end she pointed at Henry.

"Ramona, look out for your ice cream cone," Beezus warned. "You're tipping it."

That was just what Ribsy was waiting for.

With one sweep of his long pink tongue he knocked Ramona's ice cream cone to the porch. In three greedy licks the ice cream was gone. Then the cone crunched between his teeth.

Ramona let out a scream of rage.

"Look what you've done, you old dog," said Henry crossly. He looked around to see if any of the neighbors were watching. He didn't want people to say he had a dog that stole ice cream from little children.

Ribsy gave the porch a couple of licks to make sure he had not missed any ice cream. Ramona stopped screaming and started to hit Ribsy with the lunch box.

Beezus grabbed her little sister with one hand and held her own cone out of Ribsy's reach with the other. "I told you to be careful," she scolded.

"I want my ice cream cone," howled Ramona.

"Well, it's gone now," said Beezus.

Looking guilty, Ribsy slunk down the steps. He turned his back to Henry and the girls and began to gnaw an old bone in the corner of the yard.

"I want my ice cream cone," shrieked Ramona.

"Well, you can't have mine. I licked it all the way around." Beezus bit off the top of her cone and sucked out the melting ice cream. "Anyway, you were getting most of yours on your chin."

"I was not!" howled Ramona.

"Aw, I'll buy her another one," said Henry. Anything to quiet Ramona so he and Beezus could get started on their checker game. Besides, since his dog had taken the cone, he guessed he really owed her another one.

"Now?" With her grubby fist Ramona scrubbed at the tears that had rolled down into the ice cream on her chin.

"Oh, all right." Henry decided he might as well get it over with. "Wait a sec." He went into the house, where he took a dime out of a marble sack in his dresser drawer.

When Henry returned to the porch, he

118

saw Ramona walking across the lawn with her lunch box in her hand. She stopped, opened the box, and laid it on the grass. Then she ran over to Ribsy, grabbed the bone from between his paws, and put it in the lunch box. "There!" she said, as she snapped the lunch box shut.

Ribsy looked surprised. "Wuf!" he said.

"Hey," said Henry, "you can't do that."

"Ramona, you give Ribsy his bone this minute," ordered Beezus.

"No," said Ramona.

Ribsy sniffed at the lunch box. Then he looked hopefully at Ramona and wagged his tail.

"That's a camera," Henry reminded Ramona. "You can't put a bone in a camera."

"Now it's a lunch box," said Ramona.

"Ramona, give Ribsy his bone," coaxed Beezus. "Whoever heard of carrying a dirty old bone in a lunch box?"

"I have a samwidge in my lunch box." Ramona was firm. "I'm going to eat it."

"Oh, dear, now she's pretending his bone is a sandwich," said Beezus apologetically. "I don't suppose there's anything we can do about it. Maybe Mother has a bone Ribsy could have."

Henry had trouble keeping up with Ramona's thinking. At least she was quiet and that was something. "Ribsy's got lots of old bones buried around. He can dig up another one. Come on, let's go to the store and get her the ice cream cone and get it over with. I want to play checkers."

Ribsy, however, did not want another bone. He wanted the one Ramona had snatched. Sniffing at the lunch box, he trotted at Ramona's heels all the way to Glenwood School, which was across the street from the store where Henry and Beezus planned to buy the ice cream cone.

"I guess all these cars are parked here because of the P.T.A. meeting," Henry remarked, as they took a short cut across the playground. "Did your mother go?"

"No, not this time." Beezus took a Kleenex out of her pocket and tried to scrub some of the chocolate ice cream off Ramona's chin. "Mother said she was too tired after watching Ramona all day."

"I want some," announced Ramona.

"Some what?" asked Beezus.

"Some P.T.A.," said Ramona firmly.

"You can't have any P.T.A." Henry didn't see how one little girl could have so many dumb ideas. "It's the Parent-Teacher Association—just a bunch of ladies talking. Come on, we'll get you the ice cream cone."

Ramona stopped by the jungle gym on the playground. "I want some P.T.A.!" she shrieked.

"But, Ramona," protested Beezus, "how

can you have any P.T.A.? Like Henry said, it's just a bunch of ladies talking in the school auditorium and the seventh grade singing some songs for them."

"It is not," sobbed Ramona. "I want some *now*."

"What's she talking about anyway?" Henry was disgusted. All he wanted was a game of checkers and now it looked as if he had to stand around all afternoon arguing with a little kid about the P.T.A.

"I don't know what she means." Beezus sounded worried. "Come on, Ramona."

Still clutching the lunch box, Ramona threw her arms around one of the pipes on the jungle gym and screamed. Ribsy put his paw on the lunch box. Ramona snatched it from him. "Go away," she cried. "I want some P.T.A."

Ribsy gave a short bark.

"I like P.T.A.," sobbed Ramona and with

her lunch box in one hand she began to climb the jungle gym to get out of Ribsy's reach.

"You've got to find out," Henry told Beezus. "If you don't, she'll just sit there and yowl."

"I know it." Beezus sounded tired. "What do you want to do with the P.T.A., Ramona?"

"Eat it," shrieked Ramona, as she climbed higher on the jungle gym.

"Aw, how can you eat P.T.A.? I told you P.T.A. was just a bunch of ladies talking." Henry kicked at a pebble in his disgust.

"Wait a minute! Now I know what she means," exclaimed Beezus. "She thinks we're spelling something in front of her."

"How do you mean?" asked Henry.

"Well, at home when we talk about something to eat that she's not supposed to have, we spell it." Here Beezus lowered her voice to a whisper. "Like C-o-k-e and c-a-n-d-y. She thinks we're spelling something we don't want her to have. That's why she wants it."

"Oh, for Pete's sake. Leave it to Ramona." Henry could see he was not going to get to play checkers that day. "Well, now what are we going to do?"

Beezus kept her voice to a whisper. "Let's go across the street to the store and get her some cookies or something and tell her it's P.T.A."

"That's a good idea." Henry thought that for a girl Beezus was pretty sensible.

Ribsy started to follow Henry and Beezus to the store. Then he looked back at Ramona, sobbing on top of the jungle gym with the lunch box still in her hand, and decided to stay near his bone. Henry did not call Ribsy, because he knew dogs were not allowed in food stores.

Henry and Beezus looked around the

store for something that cost a dime that they could tell Ramona was P.T.A. This was not easy to do, because Ramona was familiar with cookies, popsicles, and peanuts. They finally decided on a small bag of potato chips, because Beezus was sure Ramona did not know potato chips by name and because they wouldn't drip.

When Henry and Beezus started back to the school grounds, they saw that Ribsy had his paws on the first rung of the jungle gym. "Wuf!" he said, and looked hungrily at the lunch box.

Henry also noticed two women looking at Ribsy and Ramona. One of the women was Mrs. Wisser, a friend of his mother's. She pointed to Ribsy and then to Ramona.

Now what, thought Henry, hurrying across the street. He hoped Ribsy wasn't in trouble. Not just before the fishing trip.

Mrs. Wisser was saying, "Look at the poor

little thing. She's frightened out of her wits."

"I think it's simply outrageous the way dogs are allowed to run loose in the school-yard," said the other woman. "I wonder if we dare try to pull him away so she can climb down."

"I'd be afraid to go near him," said Mrs. Wisser. "I know the dog. He belongs to the Huggins boy and I understand he's danger-ous. He bit the garbageman a week or so ago."

The Huggins boy looked at Beezus and sighed. All he wanted was to play checkers, just one little old game of checkers, and now look what had happened. How was he ever going to explain to Mrs. Wisser? And now that Mrs. Wisser thought Ribsy had chased Ramona up on the jungle gym, she would tell everybody what a dangerous dog he was. And that meant more trouble. It probably meant his father wouldn't take him fishing.

"Come on, Beezus," said Henry. "Let's try to tell her."

"Oh, there you are, Henry Huggins," said Mrs. Wisser. "Does your mother know your dog is loose on the school grounds?"

"No, Mrs. Wisser," said Henry. "She's—"

"I thought she didn't," interrupted Mrs. Wisser.

"My little sister isn't afraid of the dog," said Beezus quickly.

Ramona, who had stopped crying to listen, let out a howl. Mrs. Wisser and the other woman looked at each other and nodded.

"Wuf!" said Ribsy again.

"Henry, you hold your dog and I'll try to get her down," said Mrs. Wisser.

Henry took hold of Ribsy's collar. He wondered if Mrs. Wisser would climb the jungle gym. He hoped so. "But she's got—" he started to say.

"Don't be frightened, dear," Mrs. Wisser
called to Ramona. "We won't let the doggy
hurt you."

"Come on down, sweetheart," coaxed the
other woman.

Just then the seventh grade burst out of
the school building. Several boys began to

play a noisy game of catch. Ribsy barked excitedly.

"Hi! We've been singing for the P.T.A.," said one of the boys, as he ran past Henry.

"I want some," howled Ramona.

Ribsy grew more excited. He strained at his collar and managed to get his paws on the lower rung of the jungle gym again.

"This is outrageous," said Mrs. Wisser. "I'm going to report this dog to the principal."

"But she's got his bone," said Henry desperately.

Ramona and Ribsy and the boys playing catch made so much noise that the two women did not hear Henry. "I think the principal should call the pound and have this dog taken away," remarked the second woman, as Mrs. Wisser started toward the building.

"But he has a license," protested Henry, wishing Ribsy would not bark so much.

"What's the old garbage hound up to now?" one of the boys shouted, as he ran off to play catch.

"You shut up!" Henry yelled after the boy, who was a friend of Scooter's. "And he isn't a garbage hound!"

The doors of the school opened and the

mothers who had attended the P.T.A. meeting poured out of the building. There was such a crowd that Mrs. Wisser was unable to enter.

"Quick, get her down," Henry begged Beezus. If only they could get Ramona down and go home before Mrs. Wisser got back!

"Ramona, here's your P.T.A.," said Beezus, waving the bag of potato chips. "Come down and get it."

"No," said Ramona.

"Ramona Geraldine Quimby, you come down this instant," ordered Beezus. "You come down or you can't have any P.T.A."

"Can't you climb up and get her?" Henry was desperate. What if Miss Mullen, the principal, really did call the pound?

Beezus started up the jungle gym. "You just wait, Ramona. I'm going to tell Mother on you."

Ramona began to shriek all over again.

This excited Ribsy, who barked harder than ever and attracted the attention of some of the mothers, who walked over to the jungle gym to see what the commotion was about.

"Shut up, Ribsy," ordered Henry. "Can't you see the trouble you're getting into?"

"How can I get her down?" Beezus asked. "I can't carry her down and if I pry her loose, she might fall."

"Why, the little girl is afraid of the dog," one of the mothers said.

"No, she isn't." Henry spoke up, but no one paid any attention to him. They were all looking at Ramona.

"She's so frightened she's crying," someone said. "Look at her little face all streaked with tears."

And chocolate ice cream, thought Henry.

"I think it's a shame a little girl can't play on the school grounds without being annoyed by a dog," said another mother.

"My dog isn't annoying her. She's annoying him." Henry tried to explain the situation to the mother nearest him, but she looked at him as if she did not believe he was telling the truth.

"Maybe we should discuss this at the next P.T.A. meeting," someone suggested.

"Next meeting! We'd better do something now," said another mother. "It's the Huggins dog. One of my neighbors says she has a terrible time with him because he sits and waits for her cat to come out of the house so he can chase it up a tree."

Henry wished he and Ribsy could disappear. Now all the mothers in the whole school would think Ribsy was awful.

"Do you think we should call the police?" someone asked.

"Oh, I wouldn't do that," said one of the mothers. "I know that little Ramona Quimby. She's a perfect terror."

Henry felt better. At least he had one friend in the crowd.

"Well, really," said another mother, "just because the poor little thing is too young to have established acceptable behavior patterns doesn't mean we can let her be terrified by that dog."

Henry did not know what the lady meant but he felt it didn't sound very good for Ribsy.

"I think we should call the pound," someone said. "You can see how frightened she is."

"Why, Henry!" It was Mrs. Huggins. "What on earth is happening?"

"His dog chased that little girl up on the jungle gym and won't let her come down," explained one of the women, before Henry could open his mouth.

Mrs. Huggins glanced at Ramona and then looked sympathetically at Henry. "He's not a vicious dog," she told the woman.

"Mom, he didn't chase her. Honest," said Henry.

Then Mrs. Wisser, followed by Miss Mullen, the principal, pushed her way through the crowd of mothers. "There's the dog," Mrs. Wisser said, pointing at Ribsy.

Miss Mullen! thought Henry. Now I suppose I'll really catch it. Miss Mullen was nice, but when she said something she meant it.

Miss Mullen was tall and gray-haired. When she spoke, other people listened. "Hello, Henry, what's the trouble?" she asked pleasantly. The other women stopped talking.

Feeling uneasy, Henry looked around at all the mothers. He licked his lips and began. "Well, it looks like my dog chased Ramona up the jungle gym, but he didn't really." Henry gulped and went on. "She took his bone away from him and put it in her lunch box and he just wants his bone back, is all." Henry decided it was not necessary to tell about the ice cream cone.

"That's right, Miss Mullen," said Beezus, from the middle of the jungle gym.

"I have a samwidge in my lunch box," screamed Ramona.

"But the child was obviously frightened," said Mrs. Wisser. "She was crying as if her little heart would break."

"She was crying before she climbed up there," said Beezus.

"I'm sure Ribsy wouldn't hurt anyone," said Miss Mullen.

Henry was surprised to learn that the principal knew his dog's name.

Miss Mullen smiled. "We all know Ribsy very well at Glenwood School," she said. "He meets Henry under the fir tree every day after school. I've been watching him from my office window for a long time and he has never annoyed any of the children. In fact, he's unusually good-natured." Then Miss Mullen looked up at Ramona. "You may come down now," she said, pleasantly but firmly.

Ramona scowled but she climbed down.

"Now give Ribsy his bone," said Miss Mullen.

Ramona looked sulky as she unfastened the lunch box and handed Ribsy his bone. He took it in his mouth and looked at Henry as if to say, "Can't we go home now?"

The crowd of mothers, some looking a little embarrassed, began to drift away.

"Thank you, Miss Mullen," said Mrs. Huggins.

"Gee, thanks, Miss Mullen," said Henry gratefully. "I didn't know what I was going to do. They were going to send Ribsy to the pound."

Miss Mullen smiled. "That's all right, Henry. I understand. I have three dogs of my own at home, you know."

"You do?" Henry was astounded. Miss Mullen with three dogs! He had never thought of her as having any life outside Glenwood School at all. But three dogs!

As the principal went back into the building, Beezus took a Kleenex out of her pocket and held it to Ramona's nose. "Blow," she said. Ramona blew.

"It really wasn't Ribsy's fault," Beezus said to Mrs. Huggins.

Henry's mother smiled. "I understand."

Then Beezus handed her little sister the potato chips. "Here's your P.T.A.," she said crossly. "I hope you're satisfied."

Mrs. Wisser, however, did not give up easily. "I know you're fond of the dog," she said to Mrs. Huggins, "but he really did frighten the child." Then she squatted down on her heels so she could look into Ramona's face. "Did the doggy frighten you, dear?" she asked.

"No," said Ramona, staring at Mrs. Wisser. Then she squatted down on her heels, too. Henry thought this made Mrs. Wisser look very silly. Ramona stuffed another potato chip into her mouth as Mrs. Wisser hastily stood up. "I *like* P.T.A.," announced Ramona.

"I just bet you do," said Henry. "Come on, Beezus. If we hurry, maybe we'll have time for one game of checkers before dinner." And then because he knew his fishing trip was safe, Henry began to sing, "Woofies Dog Food is the best."

Beezus joined him on the second line and together they sang, "Contains more meat than all the rest!"

6
Ribsy Goes Fishing

I can't find my tin pants," Mr. Huggins announced Friday evening after supper.

"Dad!" shouted Henry. When his father got out his tin pants, which were not tin at all but heavy canvas, Henry knew it meant only one thing. His father was going fishing—salmon fishing. "I get to go, too, don't I? Don't I, Dad?"

Mr. Huggins grinned at Henry. "Think

you can get up at three in the morning?"

"Sure, I'll get up! Boy, oh, boy, I bet I catch a bigger salmon than anybody!"

"I wouldn't count on it," said Mr. Huggins. "I'm afraid a twenty- or thirty-pound chinook would be too much for you to handle."

"Aw, I bet I could land one," boasted Henry. After all, if he could lift Robert when they practiced tumbling, a twenty-five-pound fish couldn't be so heavy. He could see himself having his picture taken with his salmon in one hand and his rod in the other. Well, maybe he couldn't hold up such a big fish with one hand but he could prop it up some way.

"Henry," Mrs. Huggins looked thoughtfully at her son, "you mustn't be too disappointed if you don't catch anything."

"I won't, Mom, but I just know I'll catch a salmon." Henry patted his dog, who was dozing in front of the fireplace. "Did you hear that, Ribsy? We're going fishing!"

"Hey, who said anything about Ribsy?" asked Mr. Huggins.

"Aw, Dad, he wouldn't be any trouble," protested Henry. "Would you, fellow?" Ribsy opened one eye and looked at Henry.

"If Henry is old enough to go fishing, so is Ribsy," said Mrs. Huggins. Then she smiled and said, "Tomorrow is my vacation. I'll pack your lunches tonight and you can get your own breakfast. I'm going to sleep late and I don't want to have to get up to let Ribsy in and out."

"All right, Ribsy goes fishing," agreed Mr. Huggins.

"Where are we going?" Henry wanted to know.

"I thought we'd try our luck at the mouth of the Umptucca River," answered Henry's father.

"That's where Scooter went last week," remarked Henry.

"Henry, you'd better run along to bed if you're going to get up at three in the morning," said Mrs. Huggins. "And be sure you wear warm clothes tomorrow. It will be cold over on the coast."

For once Henry did not object to going to bed early. Even so, it seemed as if it were still the middle of the night when his father woke him. They could see the stars shining as they ate a hurried breakfast, standing at the draining board. When Ribsy padded into the kitchen to see what was going on, Henry gave him half a can of Woofies and some horse meat.

The Grumbies' screen door slammed. "Get your rain hat and coat and let's go." Mr. Huggins picked up two lunch boxes from the kitchen table and hurried out the back door.

"So you're going with us," said Mr.

Grumbie, when he saw Henry.

"Yes, and I bet I catch a salmon," answered Henry.

"Better not count on it," said Mr. Grumbie, and yawned. He frowned when he saw Ribsy getting into the backseat of the Huggins car with Henry, but he yawned again and did not say anything.

As they drove out of the city, Henry listened to his father and Mr. Grumbie talk about fish they had caught on other fishing trips. Ribsy could not decide where he wanted to ride. He jumped from the back seat to the front seat. He walked across Mr. Grumbie's lap and wagged his tail in his face. When Mr. Grumbie did not lower the window for him, Ribsy scrambled into the backseat and bounded from one side of the car to the other, until Henry opened a window so he could lean out and sniff all the interesting smells.

Mr. Grumbie turned around and frowned

at Ribsy. He did not say anything. He just turned up the collar of his mackinaw.

"Henry, it's pretty cold for an open window," said Mr. Huggins.

"OK, Dad." Henry pulled Ribsy back into the car by his collar and wound up the window. Ribsy turned around three times, curled up on the seat, and went to sleep.

Mr. Grumbie told about the big one that got away down on the Nehalem River. I bet I do catch a salmon, Henry thought, and using Ribsy for a pillow he fell asleep himself.

Henry did not wake up until the car left the highway and began to bounce along a gravel road near a bridge that bore a sign, "Umptucca River." The sky was gray and the air smelled of the sea. "Is it time for lunch?" Henry asked.

"Here we are," said Mr. Huggins, "and it is exactly six A.M."

Henry got out of the car and looked around. In the dim morning light he could see a shabby building with "Sportsmen's Cannery" painted across the front, a tiny restaurant with steamy windows, a few cabins, and a boathouse with a sign, "Mike's Place. Boats and Tackle." The sound of the breakers and the sight of the rows of boats bobbing in the river below the boathouse filled Henry with excitement. He was really here. He was really going salmon fishing.

While Mr. Huggins rented a boat, Ribsy ran in circles sniffing all the strange new smells. Henry examined the scales hanging from the eaves of the boathouse. He took hold of the hook and pulled down until the hand of the scales spun around and pointed to twenty-five pounds. It sure takes a lot of pulling to make twenty-five pounds, thought Henry. More than anything he wanted to hang a salmon on that hook and see the hand point to twenty-five—or maybe even thirty. He would have his picture taken with his salmon hanging on the scales so everyone would know how much it weighed.

"I brought my boy along this time," Mr. Huggins said to Mike, the owner of the boathouse.

"Well, hello there, Shorty," said Mike. "So they're going to make a fisherman out of you."

"Yes, sir. I hope I catch a salmon," answered Henry, and when he saw Mike's smile he was sorry he had said it. Maybe everyone was right. Maybe he couldn't land a salmon even if one did bite. Still, there wasn't any harm in hoping he could, was there?

"Fishing pretty good?" asked Mr. Huggins.

"Pretty good," Mike answered. "Fellow brought in a thirty-six-pounder yesterday."

Thirty-six pounds! Oh, boy, thought Henry, as he took the lunches and followed his father and Mr. Grumbie down the steps to a boat tied to a float in the river. Ribsy followed Henry into the boat and sniffed at the lunches.

"Wind from the south. Going to rain," remarked Mr. Grumbie, as he wound the rope around the starter and yanked it. The motor sputtered and was silent. Mr. Grumbie rewound the rope.

Hurry, thought Henry. I want to get started fishing.

Mr. Grumbie yanked the rope again. This

time the motor started. Henry turned up the collar of his raincoat against the wind and hung onto the side of the boat. The river looked cold and deep. Ribsy stood in the bow and barked excitedly at the seagulls wheeling overhead, as their boat joined the other boats scurrying toward the sandbars at the mouth of the river.

Although the Umptucca was several hundred feet wide at Mike's Place, it was much narrower where it ran into the ocean, because sandbars had formed on either side of the river's mouth. Mr. Grumbie anchored the boat just inside the sandbars in line with the boats already there. Henry knew this was the best spot to catch the fish as they came out of the ocean and started up the river to spawn.

"Golly," said Henry, as he watched the swift current of the river seethe against the breakers, "it looks like the river is fighting to get into the ocean and the ocean is fighting to get into the river. I wouldn't want to fall in and get carried out there."

Mr. Huggins and Mr. Grumbie did not answer. They were too busy getting out the tackle. Mr. Huggins handed Henry a stout rod with a reel attached. The end of the line was fastened to one corner of a three-cornered piece of plastic. A lead sinker was joined to another corner and from the third corner hung a piece of wire with a hook, some red feathers, and a glittering piece of brass.

"Henry, I think the easiest way for you to fish is to drop your line overboard and let the current carry it out," said Mr. Huggins. "Like this." He tossed the line into the water. The reel on the rod began to spin as the line was carried out.

"But you didn't bait the hook," said Henry.

"Salmon that are trying to get up the river to spawn aren't hungry," explained Mr. Huggins. "They bite because the brass spinner makes them angry."

"Oh," said Henry. He hoped he could make a salmon good and angry. Then he said, "Ribsy, you get away from those lunches."

Henry and the two men settled down to fish in silence. Henry dropped his line overboard, let it be carried out, and slowly reeled it in. His father and Mr. Grumbie, skillful fishermen, threw their lines out.

Henry dropped his line again and again. The wind grew colder and his nose began to run. Toss out the line, reel it in, wipe his nose. Toss out the line, reel it in, wipe his nose. Finally he said, "Dad, is it lunchtime yet?"

Mr. Huggins looked at his watch. "It is exactly eight thirty-six."

Toss out the line, reel it in, wipe his nose. Henry tried not to think about how hungry he was. Ribsy sniffed at the lunches and looked hopefully at Henry.

A shout went up from another boat, and Henry looked in time to see a man lean out of his boat and hook a great silvery fish through the gills with his gaff and pull it into his boat.

"Must be a twenty-pounder," remarked Mr. Grumbie, as the line sang from his reel.

Henry was filled with excitement at the sight of the great fish. Come on, salmon, bite, he thought, and tossed out his line.

Large raindrops began to splash the boat. Then the rain came pelting down. Rivulets of water ran off Henry's rain hat. Ribsy shivered and whimpered. Toss out the line, reel it in, wipe his nose. Henry began to wonder if salmon fishing was so much fun after all. If only he was not so hungry.

Finally when the rain stopped Mr.
Huggins said, "What do you say we knock
off for a few minutes and have a sandwich?"

"Suits me," said Mr. Grumbie.

"Boy, am I starved!" Henry reached for
his lunch box. He poured some soup from

his thermos and bit into a thick ham sandwich. Mmm, did it taste good! Ribsy watched every bite he took. When Henry swallowed, Ribsy swallowed. Poor Ribsy. He looked so thin with his wet hair plastered against his body. Henry gave him half a sandwich.

"Save some lunch for later," warned Mr. Huggins. "We have a long day ahead of us."

Ribsy gulped the bread and meat. Then he stood up and shook himself so hard his license tags jingled. Water showered in every direction, spattering faces, soaking sandwiches, splashing into the coffee the men were drinking from their thermos tops.

"Hey, cut that out!" Mr. Huggins tried to hold his sandwich out of the spray.

Mr. Grumbie did not say anything. When Ribsy stopped shaking, he pulled out a handkerchief and mopped his face. Then he poured his coffee into the river, stuffed his sandwich back into his lunch box, and got out another.

Mr. Grumbie sure is fussy, thought Henry, taking a big bite out of his soggy sandwich, while Ribsy sat in front of him and watched hungrily. He wagged his tail to show he would like another bite. His tail slapped against the tackle box. Before Henry could grab it, the box turned over, spilling spinners, hooks, and sinkers into the water in the bottom of the boat.

"That sure was close," exclaimed Henry, looking at the tangle of tackle. "Ribsy might have got a fishhook in his tail. That would have been awful."

Mr. Grumbie cleared his throat. "Uh, yes," he said, and bent to unsnarl the tackle.

"Henry," said Mr. Huggins quietly, "you'd better keep an eye on Ribsy."

"I'm sorry, Dad." Henry felt uncomfortable. Of course Mr. Grumbie didn't like

Ribsy's overturning the tackle box. But just the same it would have been awful if Ribsy had got a fishhook in his tail.

Henry looked at his wet dog shivering in the wind. "Here, Ribsy, get under my raincoat." He made a place for Ribsy, who managed to turn around three times before he curled up on the narrow seat and went to sleep. At least he can't get into trouble when he's asleep, thought Henry, and wolfed a third sandwich, the rest of his soup, a deviled egg, a piece of chocolate cake, and a banana.

The warm soup and the rocking of the boat made Henry sleepy. He tossed out his line, reeled it in, and wiped his nose over and over again. Why couldn't a fish hurry up and bite? He wished he could go back to the boathouse and stretch his legs, but he didn't like to say so when his father and Mr. Grumbie were so interested in fishing. Occasionally a shout went up from one of the other boats and someone held up a salmon. Rain clouds washed over the forest-covered mountains along the edge of the sea. To the south Henry could see another shower approaching. He turned up the collar of his raincoat and waited for the first drops to come spattering down.

"What time is it, Dad?" Henry asked.

"Ten o'clock," answered his father, reeling in his line. "Getting tired?"

"N–no." Henry tried to keep from shivering. Only ten o'clock in the morning. It seemed as if they had been there forever. Why, it wasn't even lunchtime! If only he could put his head down someplace for just a few minutes . . .

Suddenly Mr. Grumbie uttered a noise that sounded like "Wup!"

"Got something?" Mr. Huggins's voice was tense as he put down his rod and picked up the gaff.

"Yup." Grimly Mr. Grumbie wound his reel.

Henry was no longer sleepy. He dropped his rod and watched eagerly as Mr. Grumbie reeled in his line. He wanted to see exactly how a fish was landed. If a salmon bit for Mr. Grumbie, a salmon might bite for him.

Mr. Grumbie stopped winding the reel. The line began to unwind and Henry knew the salmon was pulling on it. "Is it going to get away?" Henry whispered to his father. He knew he must not disturb Mr. Grumbie.

"I don't think so," answered Mr. Huggins. "If the fish puts up a fight, it's best to let him have the line or he'll break it."

When Mr. Grumbie began to wind the reel again, Henry watched breathlessly. Suddenly the fish began to fight once more. Mr. Grumbie looked grim as he waited for the salmon to rest. Then he turned the handle of the reel again. The great fish flopped out of the water near the boat. "Get him!" said Mr. Grumbie.

Henry watched his father lean out of the boat with the gaff. "Got him," he said, as he hooked the fish through the gills and yanked it into the boat. The enormous fish did not stop fighting. Mr. Huggins tried to club it but missed, and the flopping salmon slapped against the sleeping Ribsy.

Ribsy woke up, saw the strange flopping thing, gave one terrified yelp, and tried to scramble away from it. As he fell over the line and fought desperately to get away, the hook was torn from the salmon's mouth. Mr. Grumbie tried to grab his fish, but it slid through his hands, leaving them covered with scales. Again it slapped against Ribsy, who fell over the lunch boxes in his struggle to get away. With one mighty flop the fish cleared the side of the boat, landed with a splash that showered Henry and the two men, and swam away.

"Ki-yi-yi," yelped the terrified Ribsy, as he fought free of fishing rods and lunch boxes. With one frantic glance backward, he leaped out of the other side of the boat and started swimming upstream.

It all happened so fast that Henry and the two men sat with their mouths open.

"Well . . ." said Mr. Huggins.

Mr. Grumbie did not say a word. He looked at his hands, covered with fish scales, and stared at the water where his fish had disappeared.

"Dad, start the boat," yelled Henry. "Get Ribsy. He'll be carried out to sea."

It seemed to Henry that it took his father forever to pull up the anchor and wind the rope around the starter. "Ribsy!" he called frantically to his dog, who was fighting against the swift current of the river with his nose pointed out of the water. "Dad, hurry!" Henry knew that if Ribsy was carried into the breakers he wouldn't have a chance.

Mr. Huggins jerked the rope. The motor sputtered and died. Hurriedly he rewound the rope.

"Dad!" cried Henry in despair. "Ribsy!" The dog was swimming with all his strength but was slowly being carried backward. A gust of wind blew across the choppy water and a wave washed over Ribsy's head.

Still the boat would not start.

"Dad, he can't swim against that current," cried Henry, looking back at the hungry breakers. "Can't you hurry?"

Mr. Huggins rewound the rope and yanked. The motor gave a tired gasp.

Now Ribsy was being carried back past the boat. I've got to get him, thought Henry, and leaned out of the boat. Ribsy was so close he could see the wild look in his eyes and watch his paws working under the water. Henry leaned a little farther out of the boat, reached toward Ribsy, and lost his balance. As he started to topple into the water he felt a hand grab him by the collar of his raincoat and yank him back into the boat.

"Don't lean out," said Mr. Huggins sharply, and rewound the rope. Henry knew there was no reason now to lean out of the boat. The current had swept Ribsy far beyond his reach.

By this time the fishermen in the other boats were watching. "Don't worry, sonny," called one of the men. He pulled up his anchor, started his powerful motor, and headed toward Ribsy. More terrified than ever by the roar of the motor, Ribsy struggled to get away from the boat bearing down on him.

Henry was almost afraid to look. What if the man couldn't catch Ribsy? Or what if

the boat ran over him? The man steered his boat close to Ribsy, reached out with his gaff, hooked it through Ribsy's collar, and lifted the struggling, dripping dog into his boat.

The other fishermen began to laugh. "Must be a thirty-pounder you just landed," someone called.

Henry was limp with relief. Let them laugh. Ribsy was safe. He wasn't going to be carried out into those angry breakers. That was all that mattered.

The man swung his boat around in a wide circle and pulled up close to the Hugginses' boat. He handed the soggy dog across to Henry.

"Gee, thanks," Henry managed to say, as he clutched the shivering Ribsy.

"Don't mention it," answered the man. His big boat roared away, leaving the smaller boat bobbing in its wake.

"Gee . . ." Henry hugged his dog. Ribsy licked his face with his long pink tongue. "Gee, that sure was close."

"It sure was," agreed Mr. Huggins. An uncomfortable silence fell on all three. "Sorry about the salmon, Grumbie," added Mr. Huggins.

"Must have been a twenty-five-pounder," said Mr. Grumbie regretfully.

Henry didn't want to look at Mr. Grumbie. "I'm sorry, too," he said, as he ran his hand along Ribsy's tail to wipe off some of the water. "I guess Ribsy had never seen a salmon before and it scared him. I know he didn't mean to make you lose it."

"Henry, how would you like to take Ribsy to the boathouse to dry out?" asked his father.

"Good idea," said Mr. Grumbie.

"OK, Dad," agreed Henry, because he wanted to get his dog warm and dry again.

But from the way Mr. Grumbie spoke he knew he would have to stay there the rest of the day. And his chance to catch a salmon was gone. Henry looked sadly at his dog.

Ribsy stood up and shook himself until his license tags jingled.

7

Henry's Adventure

Well, I guess it wasn't your fault."
Henry looked glumly at Ribsy,
huddled in front of the electric heater in
Mike's boathouse. It did seem as though his
dog got him into a lot of trouble. Now, after
all his bragging, he wouldn't get to take a
salmon home to show people. As for Mr.
Grumbie—Henry did not like to think
about the long ride home in the same car

with him. He knew Mr. Grumbie would be thinking about his lost salmon and blaming it on Ribsy.

Henry looked out of the window at the scales hanging from the eaves and sighed. Because of Ribsy he had lost his chance to hang a fish on that hook and watch the hand spin around to twenty-five.

"What time is it?" Henry asked the boat-house man.

"Five after two," answered Mike.

Five minutes past two. It would be at least three hours before his father would be through fishing, and Henry had eaten all his lunch hours ago—with Ribsy's help, of course. He wished he had some money so he could go across to the restaurant and buy a hamburger.

Henry amused himself looking at the pictures of fishermen with their catches that covered the walls of the boathouse. He examined a case full of tackle for sale. Then he looked through a telescope that stood by a window. He focused it on his father and Mr. Grumbie, but he couldn't see any salmon in their boat. If Mr. Grumbie should catch a whopper, the ride home would not be so bad.

Henry turned the telescope on the other boats. If some of the other fishermen were pulling in salmon, maybe Mr. Grumbie would land one, too. When Henry came to the last boat in line he looked, twisted the adjuster, and looked again. Was that Scooter McCarthy and his father? It looked like them, but the brims of their hats were turned down so far Henry could not be sure. Lots of men wore black raincoats and almost every boy had a yellow slicker, so it might be somebody else. Henry hoped so. If he had to watch Scooter come in lugging a salmon, even a silverside, he didn't know what he would do.

"Smells kind of doggy in here, doesn't it?" remarked Mike.

"My dog is almost dry," answered Henry, as he rubbed his foot through a puddle of water that had dripped off Ribsy.

A man came in to buy some tackle. He sniffed and looked around. "I thought it smelled like wet dog in here," he said, when he saw Ribsy.

Henry began to feel uncomfortable, almost unwelcome.

Two women came in to look at their husbands through the telescope. They glanced at Ribsy and frowned. "I don't think there's anything that smells quite so bad as a wet dog," said one of the women, as she adjusted the telescope.

"Come on, Ribsy, let's go outdoors." Henry didn't think Ribsy smelled so bad— just a little extra doggy, was all. But if they weren't wanted, well, they'd wait someplace else. Henry sighed and wondered what they would do the rest of the long afternoon. It wouldn't be so bad if only he was not so hungry.

Outside, Henry looked over the row of parked cars. Third from the end he found a green two-door Ford, deluxe model, with nylon seat covers, a Yellowstone National Park sticker on the windshield, and a Mount Rainier National Park sticker on the rear window. There could be no doubt about it. That car surely belonged to Scooter's father.

"Let's go down to the beach," Henry said to his dog. "Then maybe we won't have to see old Scooter when he comes in with all those fish he'll probably catch. You'd think with the whole Pacific Ocean full of fish he could have gone someplace else."

The rain had stopped and the wind blew ragged clouds across the blue sky. Henry and his dog followed a sandy road that wound through piles of driftwood—logs and stumps, boards and boxes, all bleached gray by the sea—until they came to the hard wet sand along the breakers. Henry looked at the people fishing from the sandbars and then wandered along the beach. He threw sticks into the breakers to see them carried up on the sand and then get sucked back into the ocean by the undertow. He picked up a few shells and examined a jellyfish lying on the sand. And all the time he was thinking about the salmon he wouldn't catch and wondering how he could face Mr. Grumbie on the way home.

"Come on, Ribsy, race you!" Henry called above the roar of the surf. Ribsy stopped trying to chase seagulls. Leaving a border of paw prints along the edge of the waves, he ran up the beach ahead of Henry.

Henry began to enjoy himself. He made a game of seeing how close to the water he could run without letting the waves touch his shoes. Gradually the sun sank toward the ocean, and Henry knew it would not be long before his father and Mr. Grumbie would be through fishing for the day. He decided it was time to start back to the boathouse. "Here, Ribsy," he called.

Ribsy paid no attention. He was barking

furiously at something Henry could not see.

What's the matter with him, Henry wondered. He's sure excited about something. Must be another jellyfish. Maybe I better go look at it.

Ribsy was standing at the edge of a small stream. When Henry got there, he looked into the stream to see what was making the dog bark. Then he stopped in his tracks and stared. It wasn't true. It couldn't be. But there it was! In the shallow water at Henry's feet an enormous chinook salmon was trying to fight its way upstream.

"Wow!" exclaimed Henry, as he watched the salmon struggle to swim in water that barely covered its silver body. The fish was so close he could see the pattern of its scales and the needle-sharp teeth in its mouth. I bet he took a wrong turn, thought Henry. I bet he thinks this is the river. Oh, why did I leave my tackle in the boat? Why didn't

I bring it with me?

The weary salmon rested and the current of the stream carried it back toward the ocean. Then it started fighting its way upstream again.

I've got to get him, thought Henry. I've just got to, that's all.

But how? He didn't even have a string and a bent pin, and if he did they wouldn't be any good for such a big fish. He looked around the beach for something he could use to catch the salmon.

Once more the chinook was carried back toward the ocean.

Come on, keep fighting, thought Henry. Don't give up. I've got to think of a way to get him before someone comes along and beats me to it.

Without bothering to take off his shoes, Henry stepped into the stream and waded out to the salmon. I wonder what's the best way to do this, he thought, and bent over. Cautiously he put his hands in the water and then with one quick movement tried to scoop the fish up onto the sand. The salmon, which was heavier than he expected, slid easily over his hands and struggled on, thrashing and fighting to get away from Henry.

Henry made up his mind he was not going to lose that fish. He flung his rain hat and coat and jacket onto the sand. I'll tackle him, that's what I'll do, he thought grimly. I've got to look out for those teeth, but maybe I can grab him by the gills.

While Ribsy continued to bark wildly, Henry took a deep breath and flung himself onto the salmon. The icy water splashed in his face and soaked through his clothes as he gritted his teeth and hugged the big, slippery fish. With one powerful lunge it twisted out of Henry's arms and tried to fight its way through water too shallow to swim in.

Dripping with water and covered with fish scales, Henry got to his feet. If I can just get him onto the sand, he thought, maybe I can sit on him. Once more he flung himself onto the fish and once more the salmon fought free and landed in still shallower water.

That's it, thought Henry. I'll keep pushing him upstream.

The next time he threw himself down he managed to get one hand into the salmon's gills, which were rough and gave him something to hang onto. Henry dug in with his knees and hung on. I think I've got him, he thought. This time the salmon didn't get away.

I *have* got him, but now what'll I do? thought Henry desperately. If I stand up and try to pick him up, he'll get away.

The weary salmon struggled. Grimly

Henry held on. His hands were numb and the stream flowing around him felt freezing cold. What'll I do? he thought. I can't hang on much longer.

Ribsy was running in circles, barking so hard he sounded hoarse. Henry could feel his grip on the fish's gills begin to slip. He's getting away, he thought miserably. I'll never be able to land him.

"Hang on!" someone yelled. Out of the corner of his eye Henry could see a man standing on the edge of the stream. Then the man disappeared.

Why did he go away, Henry wondered. Why didn't he help me? But in a moment the man reappeared with a piece of drift-wood in his hand. He waded into the stream and quickly clubbed the salmon. The fish gave one mighty flop and was still. Dripping and shivering, Henry struggled to his feet with his salmon in his arms. It was his! He had caught a chinook!

"Well, you've caught yourself a mighty fine fish," said the man. "Must weigh twenty-five pounds at least."

Henry's teeth were chattering so he could hardly speak. "Gee, th-th-thanks," he said, as he waded out of the stream. Ribsy approached the salmon cautiously. He sniffed at it. Then he backed away and barked.

"That's all right," answered the man. "I heard your dog barking and saw your raincoat on the sand. I thought something was wrong, so I came over to see what had happened." The man hung Henry's jacket and raincoat over his shoulders. "You better get dried out or you'll catch cold. Here, let me carry your salmon."

Henry didn't want to let go of his fish, but it was heavy and slippery and he was shivering so he could scarcely hang onto it.

"Yes, sir," said the man as he took the fish. "Twenty-five pounds at least."

Henry managed to grin, even though his lips were stiff with cold. "I'm sure glad my dog barked. I couldn't have managed if you hadn't come along to help me."

Boy, oh, boy, thought Henry, as he plodded across the sand in his wet clothes. Wait till the kids at home see my fish! Wait till Scooter McCarthy sees it!

As they neared the boathouse, Henry could hear the sound of motors and knew the fishermen were coming in from the river. "I think I can carry the fish now," he said, wanting to be sure everyone knew the fish was his. The man smiled as if he understood what Henry was thinking and handed him the salmon. With water dripping off his clothes and squishing out of his shoes, Henry lugged his fish toward the scales.

Several men who were waiting to weigh their catches turned to look at Henry. Mr. Huggins and Mr. Grumbie were just climbing the steps from the river. They looked tired, their faces were red from the wind and cold, and they both needed a shave. To Henry's relief, Mr. Grumbie was carrying a salmon.

"Dad, look!" called Henry, trying to keep

his fish from sliding out of his arms.

Mr. Huggins stared. Then he whistled.

"Well, look at that!" said Mr. Grumbie.

"Caught it with his bare hands," explained the man who had helped Henry. "Yes, sir, the boy waded right into that stream and tackled the fish with his bare hands. Never saw anything like it."

"And I didn't get a bite all day," said Mr. Huggins.

"Come on, let's see how much it weighs," suggested Mr. Grumbie.

Mr. Huggins helped Henry hang his fish on the scales. Henry held his breath until the hand spun around and stopped at twenty-nine pounds. *Twenty-nine pounds!* "Wow!" said Henry in a hushed voice.

Ribsy ran around the fish, barking. All the fishermen began to talk at once. "Wait a minute till I get the camera out of the car," said Mr. Huggins. "I want a picture of this."

Henry stood proudly beside his catch

while the man who had helped him told the story of how he caught the salmon all over again to the men who had just returned from the river.

Then Henry saw Mr. McCarthy and Scooter getting out of a boat at the foot of the steps. He noticed that Mr. McCarthy carried two silverside salmon. Scooter carried a lunch box.

Henry tried to look casual as Scooter and his father climbed the steps. "Hi, Scoot," he called, as Mr. Huggins returned with the camera.

"Stand close to the fish," said Mr. Huggins. He did not need to tell Henry to smile.

Henry grabbed Ribsy and made him stand at his feet. "If Ribsy hadn't barked at the salmon, I wouldn't have seen it," he explained. Ribsy kept his eye on the salmon and growled deep in his throat.

"Did you catch that fish?" demanded

Scooter, as the camera clicked.

"Sure," said Henry.

"With his bare hands," put in the man who helped Henry. "Never saw anything like it. Just waded in and tackled it with his bare hands."

"How do you like that!" muttered Scooter. "A chinook!"

"Come on, Henry," said Mr. Huggins, as he lifted the salmon off the hook. "You'd better get out of those wet clothes and wrap up in the auto robe."

"OK, Dad. So long, Scooter. See you around," Henry called, as he started toward the car. He felt sorry for Scooter standing there with his lunch box in his hand. It must be tough to fish all day and not catch anything.

Barking at the salmon, Ribsy trotted after Mr. Huggins. "Good old Ribsy," said Henry. Then he began to sing at the top of his voice:

"*Woofies Dog Food is the best,*
Contains more meat than all the rest.
So buy your dog a can today
And watch it chase his blues away.
Woof, woof, woof, Woofies!"

BEVERLY CLEARY is one of America's most popular authors. Born in McMinnville, Oregon, she lived on a farm in Yamhill until she was six and then moved to Portland. After college, as the children's librarian in Yakima, Washington, she was challenged to find stories for non-readers. She wrote her first book, HENRY HUGGINS, in response to a boy's question, "Where are the books about kids like us?"

Mrs. Cleary's books have earned her many prestigious awards, including the American Library Association's Laura Ingalls Wilder Award, presented in recognition of her lasting contribution to children's literature. Her DEAR MR. HENSHAW was awarded the 1984 John Newbery Medal, and both RAMONA QUIMBY, AGE 8 and RAMONA AND HER FATHER have been named Newbery Honor Books. In addition, her books have won more than thirty-five statewide awards based on the votes of her young readers. Her characters, including Henry Huggins, Ellen Tebbits, Otis Spofford, and Beezus and Ramona Quimby, as well as Ribsy, Socks, and Ralph S. Mouse, have delighted children for generations. Mrs. Cleary lives in coastal California.

Visit Beverly Cleary on the World Wide Web at
www.beverlycleary.com.

READ MORE ABOUT HENRY AND RIBSY IN
Henry and The Paper Route!

1

Henry's Bargain

One Friday afternoon Henry Huggins sat on the front steps of his white house on Klickitat Street, with his dog Ribsy at his feet. He was busy trying to pick the cover off an old golf ball to see what was inside. It was not very interesting work, but it was keeping him busy until he could think of something better to do. What he really wanted, he decided, was to do something different; but how he wanted that something to be different, he did not know.

"Hi, Henry," a girl's voice called, as Henry picked away at the tough covering of the golf ball. It was Beatrice, or Beezus, as everyone called her. As usual, she was followed by her little sister Ramona, who was hopping and skipping along the sidewalk. When Ramona came to a tree, she stepped into its shadow and then jumped out suddenly.

"Hi, Beezus," Henry called hopefully. For a girl, Beezus was pretty good at thinking up interesting things to do. "What are you doing?" he asked, when the girls reached his house. He could see that Beezus had a ball of red yarn in her hands.

"Going to the store for Mother," answered Beezus, as her fingers worked at the yarn.

"I mean what's that in your hands?" Henry asked.

"I'm knitting on a spool," Beezus explained. "You take a spool and drive four nails in one end, and you take some yarn and a crochet hook—like this. See?" Deftly she lifted loops of yarn over the nails in the

3

spool to show Henry what she was doing.

"But what does it make?" Henry asked.

"A long piece of knitting." Beezus held up her work to show Henry a tail of knitted red yarn that came out of the hole in the center of the spool.

"But what's it good for?" Henry asked.

"I don't know," admitted Beezus, her fingers and the crochet hook flying. "But it's fun to do."

Ramona squeezed herself into the shadow of a telephone pole. Then she jumped out and looked quickly over her shoulder.

"What does she keep doing that for?" Henry asked curiously, as he picked off a large piece of the golf ball cover. He was getting closer to the inside now.

"She's trying to get rid of her shadow," Beezus explained. "I keep telling her she can't, but she keeps trying, anyway. Mother read her that poem: 'I have a little shadow that goes in and out with me, and what can be the use of him is more than I can see.' She decided she didn't want a shadow tagging around after her." Beezus turned to her sister. "Come on, Ramona. Mother said not to dawdle."

"Oh, for Pete's sake," muttered Henry, as the girls left. Knitting a long red tail that wasn't good for anything, and trying to get rid of a shadow—the dumb things girls did! They didn't make sense. Then he looked at the battered golf ball in his hands and the thought came to him that what he was doing didn't make much sense, either. In disgust he tossed the golf ball onto the lawn.

Ribsy uncurled himself from the foot of the steps and got up to examine the golf ball. He picked it up in his teeth and trotted to the top of the driveway, where he dropped it and watched it roll down the slope to the sidewalk. Just before it rolled on into the street, he raced down and caught the ball in his mouth. Then he trotted back up the driveway and dropped the ball again.

Henry watched Ribsy play with the golf ball, and he decided that this afternoon everyone—even his dog—was busy doing something that made no sense at all. What he wanted to do was something that made sense, something important. Something like . . . something . . . Well, he couldn't think exactly what, but something *important.*

"Hi there, Henry!" A folded newspaper landed with a thump on the grass in front of Henry.

"Oh, hi, Scooter," answered Henry, glad of an excuse to talk to someone, even if it was Scooter McCarthy.

Scooter was in the seventh grade at Glenwood School, while Henry was only in the fifth. Naturally, Scooter felt pretty superior

when Henry was around. Henry looked at
Scooter sitting on his bicycle, with one foot
against the curb and his canvas bag of
*Journal*s over his shoulders.

Don't miss all six of Henry's adventures with his great dog, Ribsy!

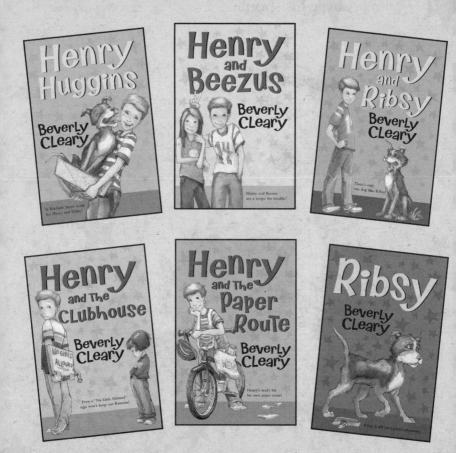